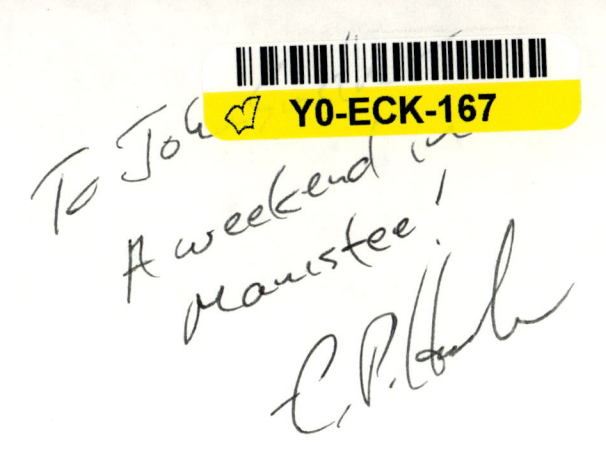

NORTHERN CR✲SS

CHRISTOPHER HUDSON

velluminous

Published by Velluminous Press
www.velluminous.com

Copyright ©2006 Christopher Hudson
www.northerncrossonline.com

The author asserts the moral right to be
identified as the author of this work.

ISBN-13: 978-1-905605-09-5
ISBN-10: 1-905605-09-9

All Rights Reserved. No part of this
publication may be reproduced, stored in a
retrieval system, or transmitted in any form or by
any means, electronic, mechanical, photocopying,
recording or otherwise, without the prior
permission of the copyright owner.

cover illustration by Elspeth Fahey

NORTHERN CROSS

For Cheryl, Linda, and Carol

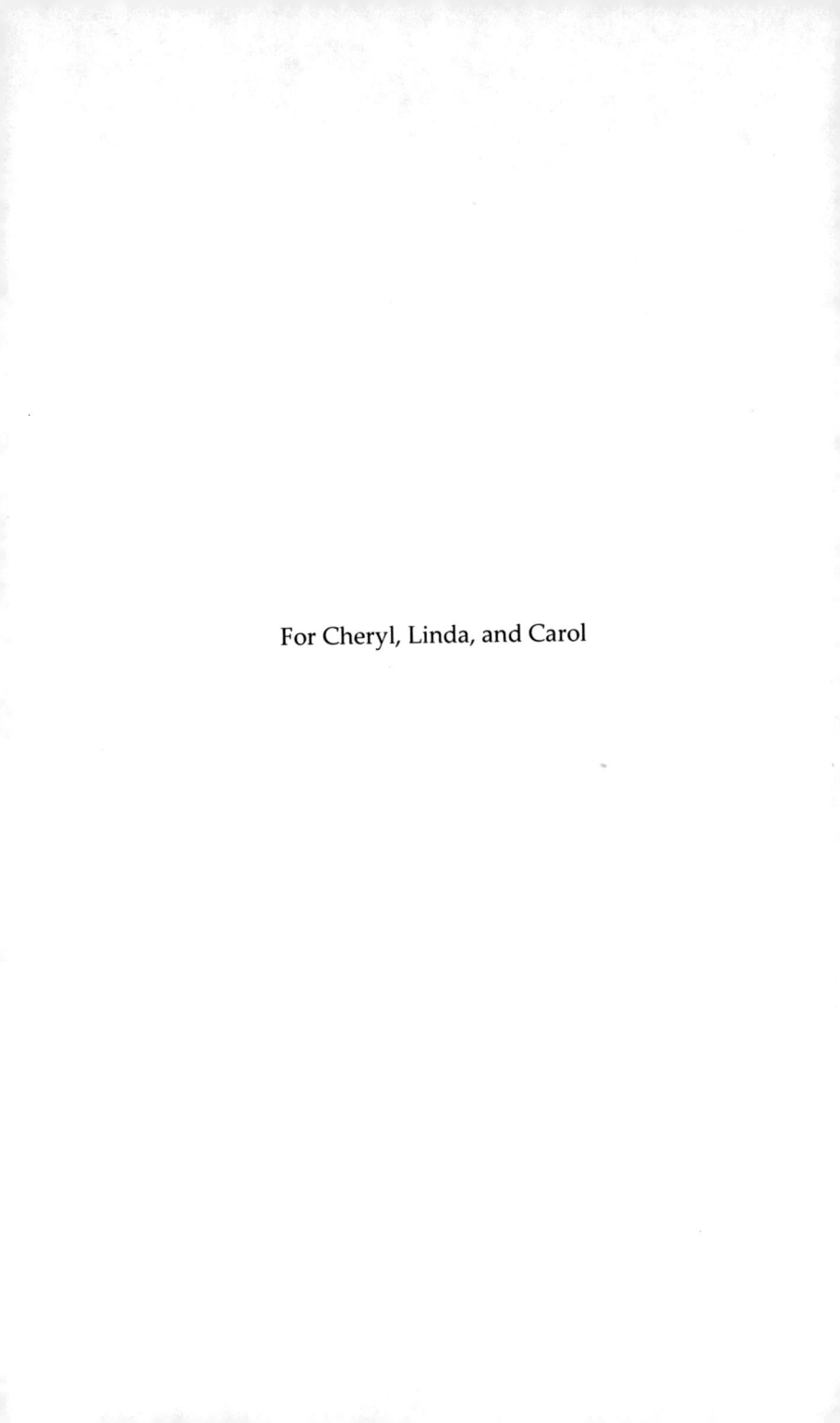

CHAPTER 1

(1970)

The flaring Zippo lighter momentarily blinded George Ashton, but illuminated the dashboard of the parked 1966 Ford station wagon. The clock read 11:10. Within seconds, the pungent odor of marijuana filled the car.

"Hey man, what the hell are you doing?" George's voice quivered with apprehension.

The man sitting next to him took a drag on the joint, so that his face became faintly visible, high cheek-bones shielding the dark eyes from the sudden smoldering glow. "What do you think I'm doing, Little Wing? Have a hit, man, it'll help you relax...you're way too uptight." Brady Keyes reached over and waved the joint under George's nose.

George pushed it away. "You're a crazy asshole, you know that, Brady?"

"Never laid any claims to the contrary." Brady drew in another big hit, held it, then continued with his exhaling breath, "Speaking of assholes, at least it wouldn't take a John Deere tractor to pull a pin out of mine."

Sudden headlights danced through bare branches to their left, imprinting an eerie spider pattern on the interior of the car. They both froze as the car paused at the stop sign before crossing the intersection in front of them.

"So, I'm a little nervous," George replied. "Anyone would

be, except for you, and it's a matter of public record that you're crazy." He watched the shrinking taillights continuing down the lonely stretch of highway, then waved the joint away. "I'd like to have a semi-clear head when this comes down, okay?"

"Fine. Far be it from me to waste good weed on an ingrate like you."

"Look, Brady, I don't mind being a foot soldier in the revolution, but this gives me the creeps. Maybe you don't feel like you have much to lose, but I do."

Brady swiveled in his seat and stabbed an accusing finger at George. "Then why the hell did you get involved with us in the first place? Why didn't you stay in the Delta Grabba Thighs, or whatever the hell you pinheads called that fraternity? You could be spending the night chug-a-lugging beers with young Republicans and pulling panty raids on sorority chicks."

"Hey, I never actually joined the Delts, I just had a few friends there. They're not all jerks."

Brady laughed and George's cheeks burned with embarrassment. "Listen, I believe in what we're fighting for," he said. "But nobody mentioned anything about highway robbery when I joined, you know?"

The other man took a final hit and exhaled. "You knew we weren't going to be playing patty-cake with the government. You volunteered for this job, as I recall, and this is our only chance to pull it off." He stubbed out the joint in the ashtray. "So quit your goddamn whining and do what you're supposed to."

"But—"

"Just be cool and everything will work out fine."

Two more cars passed through the intersection. George pulled out his own lighter and flicked it on. The clock read 11:25. "I thought they'd be here by now," he said, attempting a nonchalance he didn't feel.

"Tanya said they left the museum at ten. If they averaged fifty, they'd arrive here by 11:15, but they might have stopped for cigarettes or something. Don't worry, Little Wing, they'll be here."

"And then what?"

"Just be cool," Brady said again.

George persisted. "What are we going to do with all this art we're supposed to boost? I don't know too many people who'll buy hot impressionist paintings."

"We're told only what we need to know. We've been over that."

"Yeah, so if anybody gets caught...but you know, don't you, Brady? I know you get it on with Tanya."

"Forget it."

"If I'm going to risk my life, I'd like to know what it's for, okay?"

Brady gave him a sideways glance, then sighed. "Tanya's got a fence in Hong Kong who'll leak them slowly into the Asian market. We won't get anywhere near what they're worth, but it'll be enough to keep us in guns and butter for a while."

George shook his head. "You're crazy, you know that? And I'm crazy for being here."

"Hey, you had to know."

"Maybe I'd better check on the guys."

"Go ahead, if it'll make you feel any better."

George picked up the army surplus radio/receiver and clicked the mike button. "Green Two, Green One here, come in," he said barely above a whisper, then strained to pick out a voice above the static. "Green Two, can you hear me?"

The reply came a few seconds later, from the van parked a half-mile up the road to their left. "Yeah, George, I can hear you fine."

George heard faint laughter in the background. He turned to Brady. "I think those jerks are stoned." Brady snorted and shook his head. George couldn't tell if he was angry or laughing. He clicked on the mike again. "What are you guys doing?"

The voice on the other end choked down laughter. "Nothing, George. Just waitin' on the man, you know." Before the mike clicked off, George heard all three of them bust up.

"Damn it, Steve, if you guys are high, somebody's going to fuck up and this thing'll go down bad...can't you stay straight for two hours?"

"Hey, cool out, man. We're fine." Steve sounded quite sober until he added, "Fine as wine in the summertime," and burst out laughing.

Brady turned away from the passenger window and made a grab for the radio. "Give me that thing." He clicked on the mike. "Raimus, if you or those other two idiots do *anything* to jeopardize this mission, I will personally shoot all of you, you hear me?"

George had to strain to make out Steve's reply from the set against Brady's ear. "Don't worry, man, we're under control. We're just having a little smoke to relax. You're the one who's always saying it's the only way to cope with reality."

"I don't care if you're shooting horse. Just make sure you're up to the job. Understand?"

George heard Steve's indignant reply: "You just worry about yourselves. We'll hold up our end. Wait. Wait...hey, man, I think this might be them."

Brady clicked the mike. "You sure?"

There was a brief silence before Steve said, "This is it, Green One. Look sharp!"

※

Steve Raimus watched, wide-eyed, as an unmarked Buick sedan passed in front of their van, followed by a large delivery truck. Steve had parked facing the highway, in the shadow of a large oak tree and out of sight of the road. He set down the radio and started the engine. He didn't switch on the headlights as he pulled onto the highway behind the truck.

Sitting next him, Rick Vanbrough opened the window to get some air. "Holy shit, man! That was some righteous weed!"

Bobby Teegarten leaned forward from the back of the van. "I can't believe we're doing this. That Brady Keyes is one crazy fucker." He was shivering, maybe from the cold air being blown through the window, or maybe from the tension. "Those paintings are gonna be hotter than two-dollar pistols."

Rick could never resist an opportunity to needle Bobby. "I didn't hear you object when Tanya asked you to volunteer for this."

"Screw you, hophead," Bobby replied. "You're only here because Brady always gets the best dope."

"Shut up, you assholes," Steve snapped. "This is some heavy shit going down. Pay attention."

Following the truck, now about a hundred yards ahead, Steve saw the Buick's brake lights glow as the vehicle slowed for the stop sign. A moment later, the taillights of the truck brightened as well.

Sixty seconds after Steve announced they were rolling, George saw the headlights of two vehicles approaching the intersection. He reached for the keys dangling from the ignition of the Ford, then hesitated.

Brady leaned forward in his seat. "Come on, man. Let's go. We've got to time this perfectly."

"I want to be sure it's them."

"It's them. Let's go!" Brady leaned across, reaching for the ignition.

"All right, all right." George started the car and pulled into the intersection, then killed the motor. By the time the Buick pulled up to the stop sign, he was in front of the Ford, opening the hood.

The Buick's headlights picked out the station wagon like a floodlight. An angry voice called from behind the glare: "Get that piece-of-shit beater out of the road!"

"Hey, man, take it easy." George shaded his eyes, squinting into the headlights. "I'm not superman, you know? How about a little help pushing it to the side?"

A few seconds of silence passed, then George heard two car doors slamming.

Two uniformed security guards cut across the blinding light. "Jesus," said one of the men. "These hippies need help finding their asses in the dark." The speaker was burly, white, mid-to-late forties, and with a well-developed beer belly suspended, defiant of gravity, over his belt. The second guard was smaller, and black.

The big guy glanced at the Ford's open hood and then turned to George. "So, what's wrong?"

"I'm not exactly sure," George said.

Both men stepped up to the hood; neither noticed Brady slipping out of the passenger door. He circled around the back of the Ford and stepped into the puddle of light, shotgun leveled. "Nothing's wrong, so long as you do as you're told."

For a heartbeat, the security guards simply gaped at Brady, with his six-foot, two-hundred pound frame draped in a fatigue jacket, dark straight hair spilling from under a black stocking cap and cold eyes staring back at them.

The driver's hand dropped to his holstered pistol. "What do you think you're doing, punk?"

Brady pointed the shotgun directly at the driver's head. "Don't even think about it, unless you plan on wearing your hat on your shoulders from now on."

"Cool it, Pete," said the smaller guard. "It ain't worth it."

"Your friend's right," Brady said. "Just unbuckle your holster and let it slide to the ground. Both of you. Now." He nodded at George. "Cover them."

George pulled out the .38 special he'd been assigned and aimed it in the general direction of the guards, trying to keep the barrel from wavering. The big guy, Pete, glanced back at him and then slowly unbuckled his gun belt and let it drop. George went up from behind and kicked the holster out of reach. Pete glared. "You punks actually think you're going to get away with this?"

Brady jabbed the shotgun at him. "Shut up and do as you're told, and nobody'll get hurt."

"Fuck you, you long-haired faggot."

Ignoring the insult, Brady motioned for George to deal with the smaller guard's sidearm. As George approached, he could see a bead of sweat trickle down the black man's neck. He tightened his grip on the .38 in order to quell the trembling of his hands, keeping the pistol pointed at the guard as he scuffed the second holster away with his foot. As George looked up again, the security man glanced over his shoulder, back at the truck.

Brady noticed it, too. He yelled toward the truck. "Everything okay back there?"

For a few anxious seconds, they heard nothing. Then Steve said, "A-OK, man."

Brady yelled back, "Well, shake a leg, before more company arrives."

The interior light of the truck came on and two more guards climbed out with their hands up. Steve emerged after them, holding a pistol. He herded the men around the back of the truck.

"I didn't know any of you assholes appreciated art. I thought you just got stoned and played grab-ass with each other," Pete growled.

His partner winced. "Will you please shut up?"

"I will not shut up. These faggots ain't gonna do anything. Come on, Harlen, let's kick their asses right now." Pete glanced at George, whose hands were now shaking visibly. "See that? These pukes are scared shitless." He clenched his fists and took a step forward. "We can take 'em."

Brady flipped his shotgun, slamming the stock into the guard's jutting chin. The man staggered backwards onto the hood of the Buick, then slid to the asphalt.

Harlen started toward him. "Jesus, Pete!"

Brady shouted, "Stay put, Harlen. Show me you're not as stupid as your partner."

Steve's voice sounded from the darkness behind the truck. "Just open the goddamn door!"

Brady glanced over and jerked his head at George, though his shotgun never wavered from Harlen. "Go see what those idiots are doing."

George hurried to the truck and saw Steve holding one of the guards up against the door, his gun pressed against the base of the man's shaved skull. Bobby was scuffling with the second guard. Rick circled them both, trying to grab the guy from behind.

Steve had his target pinned, so George stepped into the fracas and thrust the .38 under the fighter's nose. "Just relax, man."

The guard gave up. "I thought you hippies were into love and peace."

George gave the man just enough attention to keep the gun pointed in the right direction. "We have to get those paintings into the van, now! Move it!"

Steve shrugged and slammed his captive against the van. "This asshole won't open the door."

The guard jerked his bald head, twisting his face away from the steel panel to which he was pinned. "You're just going to have to shoot me."

George cursed under his breath. As soon as these guys got a load of the Rick and Bobby comedy show, they'd know they were dealing with amateurs. Instinct took over—disguised as a sudden, dizzying spurt of adrenaline—and George growled, "You either open the door, or you get to clean up what's left of your partner's head." He jabbed the .38 at the fighter's skull. "Your choice."

Before the bald guy could answer, a deafening gunshot split the night, sounding from somewhere in front of the truck. A flicker of headlights signaled the approach of another car. Things were happening too fast. George's ears were still ringing from the blast, and he panicked. He hauled off with his left fist and hit the fighter, snapping the man's head back. With some surprise, he watched as his target slumped to his knees, then crumpled to the ground.

Steve still had the bald guard pinned against the rear of the truck. George yelled, "Cold cock that son of a bitch!" He turned to Rick and Bobby, both of whom were gaping like stunned trout. "Help him!"

He left them to it and ran back to the intersection. Brady and the smaller guard, Harlen, were staring at Pete, who was lying in front of the headlights with a shotgun-sized hole in his chest and blood soaking over his oversized stomach.

"What the hell happened?" George demanded.

Brady snapped, "What does it look like? The fool woke up and tried to play hero."

"Jesus, Brady."

Brady glared. "You think I should just go ahead and give Harlen my driver's license, too?"

George flicked his eyes at the approaching headlights. "There's a car coming, man. We've got to get out."

"Did they get the paintings loaded in the van?"

George shook his head. " Those truckers are putting up a fight."

"We're not leaving empty handed," Brady said. "Go get the paintings."

George glanced down the road again. "What about that car?"

"We'll make 'em help unload the truck."

"Fuck the truck," George pleaded. "We've got to go now!"

Behind them, doors slammed and an engine roared into life. Both men jerked their heads towards the sound, and George caught a brief glimpse of Steve behind the wheel of the van, squealing the tires as he threw the vehicle into reverse, then grinding into first gear and roaring around the truck toward the intersection.

Rick shouted out the passenger-side window, "We're screwed, man. We're out of here."

Brady aimed the shotgun at the van. "Get those paintings, you assholes!"

Steve leaned over to the passenger side and shouted, "Forget it, man. There's two cars coming!"

George grabbed at the barrel of the shotgun. Brady spun away from him, stepped back and aimed it directly at his chest. For a few shocked seconds, George simply stared.

"George, get in the fucking car."

As suddenly as it had come to him, the adrenaline drained away, leaving George rubber-kneed. He wanted to pass out and sleep, preferably for a week. He climbed into the station wagon and started the motor. Brady went over to Harlen and with a murmured, "Sorry, bro'," whacked him on the side of the head with the shotgun. Then he ran back to the Ford and jumped in the passenger side. "Hit it, man."

George jammed the transmission into drive and floored the gas, heading south. He glanced to his right to see the taillights of Steve's van growing fainter as the others fled to the east.

After a few minutes of silence, he spoke up. "Brady, we're college students, not highwaymen...what did you expect?"

Brady's voice was almost inhuman, and chilled him to the bone. "Just drive," he said.

Chapter 2

(1996)

Haley's Comet shuddered slightly as the landing gear locked into place.

This was going to be a bitch, George Ashton knew. With visibility at less than an eighth of a mile almost all the way down to the deck, the glowing instruments in the darkened cabin of the Beechcraft King Air C90A were all he could see. Outside the cabin windows was a formless void: no light, no indication of movement, nothing.

George twisted his head back towards the passenger section. "Sir, you'd better fasten your seatbelt, we're on final approach." His boss, Jack Haley, huddled in the small pool of light from a single reading lamp, looking over the proposal he'd received earlier that day.

Haley looked up over his half-glasses as he reached down to buckle the belt. "Not much visibility out there tonight, is there?"

"A little murky, but just routine," George lied. The lights of the city began to filter through the clouds, and he glanced at his altimeter: one thousand feet. Hoping that the instruments were more truthful than he'd just been, and that the tower was paying attention, George held to the southeasterly heading, aiming for the 5,100 foot strip of concrete known as runway fifteen of Detroit City Airport. Landing in a metropolitan airport made a night-time approach in the soup doubly hazardous.

Trying to keep the glide path and localizer needles centered, the pilot eased back on the throttles and added a touch more flap as the twin turbo-prop began to break through the overcast just over Seven Mile. A little to the west, he could see a steady stream of the northbound traffic on the Chrysler freeway, the remnants of rush hour commuters hurrying home.

The threshold of the runway appeared just ahead. George glanced down. Two hundred feet at 110 knots. His palms moistened slightly as the plane continued to descend. The runway was approaching rapidly now.

One final check of the landing gear position indicator...a belly landing would be hard on a corporate pilot's career, as well as on his plane. Everything was okay. Speed dropping to one hundred, altitude fifty feet. He chopped the power and pulled back on the yoke to begin the flare. *Haley's Comet* hesitated and bounced slightly on the pavement, and then it finally quit flying and began the long rollout.

Twenty minutes later, George was washing his face in the terminal men's room. It had been a long day. He'd left the house at 4:30 a.m. and made the hour commute from northern Oakland County into the city. By the time he'd arrived, Jack Haley was already waiting in the tiny office the company rented in the hanger near where *Haley's Comet* was kept. Didn't the man ever sleep? They were scheduled to leave for St. Louis at 6:30. Haley had already initiated the fueling process, which was an irritating usurpation of George's duty—and the sort of thing Haley did to let people know they were late.

The two-and-a-half hour flight to St. Louis had been uneventful. After seeing to the refueling and checking the weather for the return trip, George had taken a taxi to sightsee and shop for some badly needed clothes. He'd returned to the airport for the scheduled 4:00 p.m. flight, only to find a message from Haley that he wouldn't be at the airport until 6:00. That was a concern, because the weather was closing in and he didn't look forward to getting home late. Fortunately, Haley had made it in time for a 6:15 takeoff.

Three hours later, George was about to head for the parking lot and the long drive home when Ed Scripps, the night security guard, poked his head in the door. "Oh, there you are," he said.

"What's up, Ed?"

"Guy out here says he's looking for you."

"What?"

"Guy's been waiting since 6:30. I guess that's when you were due in."

"Who is he?"

Ed shrugged. "Didn't catch his name. Big guy...late forties, maybe." He thought for a moment longer. "Thin hair, slicked back." He mimed, pushing back his own thinning hair. "He's what you might call a sharp dresser."

"Thanks." George absently wiped his hands, wondering who the hell would be waiting for him. His first impulse was to slip out the back door; he was tired and not up to dealing with anybody—friend or foe. But he figured a dodge wouldn't be a particularly mature thing to do. If it were bad news, it wouldn't go away, and if it were good—it just might.

He went to the commuter passenger waiting area and looked around. At first he didn't see anyone matching the description Ed gave, but then he noticed someone standing by the window, obscured by shadows. If the man hadn't spoken first, George would have never recognized him

"Hey, Little Wing! Finally got to fly, eh?"

The voice was unforgettable: Brady Keyes.

For a moment, George felt a strong impulse to pretend Brady had the wrong guy. He fought it down and crossed the short distance between them, then grabbed the other man by the shoulders. "Holy shit, Brady! Is that really you?"

"Who'd you think it was, man? The frigging Pope?"

"Well, it's not like I run into people I haven't seen for over twenty years everyday."

"Well you have today, partner. And it's about time. Has it really been twenty years?"

It seemed more like a lifetime. George stared into Brady's eyes. He'd almost forgotten how intense those eyes were. Almost, but not quite. "I can't believe this. Where the hell have you been?"

"Hey, aren't you glad to see me, man?"

George realized that he was peering at Brady as if he were studying some kind of biology specimen. He released Brady's shoulders, grabbed his hand and pumped it furiously. "Goddamit, you look great! Come on, I think the bar's still open... let's grab a beer."

"That's more like it, Little Wing. Buy your old comrade a drink."

George stifled a shudder as he led the way to the airport lounge. No one had called him Little Wing since Brady disappeared. Not that the nickname, derived from a favorite Hendrix song, offended him; it was the implied intimacy that left him uneasy. Seeing Brady again after all these years made him realize that here was a man who had never really known him, nor really cared to.

Chapter 3

The bar was all but empty. Two businessmen nursed their drinks, staring at the large-screen TV as they waited for the last commuter to Chicago. They paid no attention as George and Brady took a corner booth. Sue, the cocktail waitress—mid-thirties, brunette, attractive but hard-looking—came to take their order.

"A little late tonight for you, ain't it, George?" The waitress's eyes darted from George to Brady and back again. "Long day?"

George smiled. "Hi, Sue. Hell of a long day. How've you been?"

"Okay, I guess. What'll you and your friend have?" She glanced at Brady Keyes again, then looked away quickly as if caught between fear and fascination. It wasn't the first time George had seen a woman react like that to his old acquaintance.

Brady smiled at her.

George said, "Couple of draughts, Sue."

"Sure, right away." She flicked her eyes once more at Brady, then turned and hurried away.

"Nice stuff, Little Wing. You make any headway with that?"

George laughed. Brady had always been the same: he could have the most beautiful girlfriend in town, and he still had to try scoring with any female that looked his way. "Sorry to disappoint you, Brady. Not my type."

"So you don't mind if I give it a go?"

"As if you need my permission," George replied. A man like Brady wasn't above hitting on his best friend's wife, let alone the casual squeeze of a casual acquaintance. "Look man, I'm damn glad to see you, but where in the hell did you come from? How did you find me?"

Brady had been checking out Sue. He checked out the rest of the bar as well, before continuing. "You wouldn't believe the trip I've been on. After that debacle on Highway 89, I figured it was every man for himself, so I split the country in a hurry. Headed South."

George flinched. Highway 89 was a memory he didn't wish to revive, but knowing Brady, they'd end up going over every painful aspect of it. That, as much as anything, was why seeing the other man again left him so uneasy.

"My brother," Brady continued, "had been living in Bogota for about a year."

"Your brother?"

"Yeah. Warren. The wild man. I don't think you ever met him."

George shook his head.

"Well, maybe you remember me talking about him? Viet Nam vet who tuned-in, turned-on, and dropped-out in a big way?"

"Vaguely." George had a dim memory of Brady discussing some invalid from his family who had gone to South America to find 'righteous dope' and live like a king on his VA pension.

"Warren had been trying to get me to come to Colombia for months. Kept raving about the drugs and the women and the good life. When the shit came down, I figured it was the best place to be...a place out of the country, with connections. What could be better?"

George wondered. His own choice had been to hide out in a small town in Montana. The guard survived Brady's gunshot, but the shooting had intensified the manhunt, particularly once Brady had been identified from fingerprints and past run-ins with the law.

The other three—Steve, Bobby, and Rick—had escaped cleanly. None of them had prior records, so the police were never able to put names with the faces.

Hiding in Montana, George had worked a series of menial jobs, winding up in a maintenance position at a small airport. There, an old love for flying had been rekindled and he traded odd jobs for flight lessons. At first, he didn't dare apply for a private pilot's license, but after a few years the authorities seemed to lose interest in tracking down the perpetrators of a failed art theft, and he took the risk. To his surprise, there was no hassle. George embraced a new career in aviation, first as a flight instructor, and then, when he had notched up enough hours and license upgrades, as a commercial pilot.

Six years later, and newly married to Julia, he'd landed the enviable position of chief pilot for Haley Electronics, a manufacturer of computer components. Since then, he'd made a decent living flying Haley VIP's around the country. George loved his job, even though spending so much time away from home put a strain on his marriage. It wasn't that Julia didn't understand his passion: she loved flying too; George had met her while instructing. But she was also anxious to start a family, and concerned that time was running out.

All in all, though, life had been good to George. Years had passed since Highway 89, enough years for him to start considering how bright and how happy his future with Julia might be.

Enough years for him to feel safe...

Until now. Now, the dumbest stunt he'd ever pulled was staring him in the face in the form of Brady Keyes. Twenty years before, George had been an innocent. He'd believed passionately in the cause of the Social Coalition. So, he'd thought, had the others. Now, with a sudden, chilling clarity, he realized that the radical leadership had been more interested in raising hell than in social consciousness, and that Brady hadn't actually cared what the cause was, as long as it gave access to excitement, good drugs and women.

"You should have come with me, Little Wing," Brady continued. "What a time we'd have had. It was more than I ever imagined, even better than Warren described." He paused, musing. "Of course he was usually too stoned to string two sentences together, but hey, that's what I mean! You can spend your whole life whacked out down there and nobody gives a shit. All they care about are your American dollars. I should have made you come."

"You look like you've done all right without me." George waved his hand, indicating Brady's designer clothes, tanned complexion and manicured nails. "It's incredible how far Warren's VA checks go."

"Hey man, Warren died eight years ago."

"I'm sorry, Brady, I didn't—"

"That's okay. How could you know? Anyway, we were doing better than living off government dole. We used the checks to snort blow. It was a big joke."

"I was only kidding, man, I figured you'd have something going on."

Brady laughed. "I fell in with the right crowd. People who know how to make things happen...who know how to live."

Something in Brady's tone made George uncomfortable; he didn't need to be a Rhodes Scholar to know what the other man meant. "So, why are you here? How did you know I was here?"

"Complete coincidence. I couldn't believe it myself. I came in on business this morning and overheard an airport employee mention your name. Naturally, I had to ask if they were talking about the George Ashton I knew. After they described your 'good looks' there was no doubt. One fellow told me when you were due back, so I came back to surprise you."

"You did that, all right. Freaked might be a better word." George took a swallow of beer. "So what's your plan? How long are you staying here?"

"Three days. I'm at the Marriott. It's decent enough, I guess."

George was tempted to let it go at that; maybe have dinner with Brady one night before he left, and that would be it. But he suspected that Brady was fishing for an offer to put him up. What the hell, why not? "No way, man. You're staying with us. Julia would never forgive me if I let an old friend stay in a hotel."

"Naw, I'm all set with a room already—"

"You've checked in?"

"No, but I've got a guaranteed late arrival."

"So, write it off. You might as well stay with us and save the other two nights."

"You sure it'd be okay with the ol' lady?"

"She's heard all about you. I know she'd like to meet you. I'll never hear the end of it if she found out you were in town and I didn't make you come home with me." George drained his glass and set it back on the table. "Besides, I want you to meet her." He laughed to himself at that one. If he didn't trust Julia implicitly, he wouldn't let Brady within ten miles of her. "I'll just call ahead to let her know we're coming."

Chapter 4

With Brady following in his rented car, the ride to George's modest home in one of the few remaining blue-collar neighborhoods near Rochester seemed to take longer than usual. Memories flooded into his mind: scenes he could see with crystal-clarity, things that he'd not thought about in years.

Some he remembered fondly. Others haunted him.

Approaching home, familiar surroundings brought him back to the present. Rochester had once been a sleepy little farming community, but now it was sucking in yuppie dollars. Old farms gave way to developments of 4,000 square-foot houses; shot-and-a-beer saloons became happy-hour fern-bars; quaint stores, once frequented by farmers looking for supplies, became up-scale specialty shops drawing in tastefully dressed young mothers who had just dropped off the kids for tennis or riding lessons.

These changes weren't necessarily bad, as far as George was concerned. It was just that the relentless quest for lifestyle was depressing. People seemed to be constantly looking for something—for the right house or the neighborhood that would bring them happiness, for the newest fashion or fad that would make their life complete. In the meantime, the obsessive seekers lived without love or passion or laughter.

As he pulled into his driveway, George became embarrassingly aware of his own sellout to consumerism. The modest brick ranch looked just like his parent's home in the middle-class neighborhood where he grew up. Brady noticed too. When he mentioned it, George comforted himself with the thought that the apple hadn't fallen far from Brady's family tree either: his father had been a smalltime bookmaker on the fringes of organized crime.

Inside, they were greeted by the unmistakable sound of a television show in progress. A moment later, Julia appeared in the entrance hall and welcomed her husband with a hug and a kiss. Then she turned to Brady and held out her hand. "It's so nice to meet one of George's old friends. He doesn't like talking about the past." Her piercing blue eyes didn't waver as she studied Keyes. "Maybe I'll get the chance to discover a different side of him."

Brady glanced around the hallway, then returned his gaze to Julia. "It seems to me, Mrs. Ashton, that his past is nowhere near as interesting as his present." He actually looked uncomfortable under Julia's intense gaze, for a second or two. Then the laugh track of the sitcom she'd been watching kicked in, and the moment was past.

"Please, call me Julia." Her words were friendly, but her voice held a cool quality. So did her eyes.

"Of course, Julia." Brady laughed, for no particular reason that George could see. He seemed nervous—uncharacteristically so. "I hope I'm not inconveniencing you?"

George found himself enjoying Brady's discomfort. Julia had the most open and unpretentious manner he had ever encountered. He too had wilted under the piercing scrutiny of those blue eyes, but he'd always been a little insecure around women anyway. To see Julia at work on a renowned womanizer like Brady Keyes was a hoot.

A smile transformed Julia's face, and George wondered what had amused her, what subtle humor he'd failed to detect.

"Come in, Brady," she said. "Let me take your coat." She accepted the jacket and turned to hang it in the closet. "George, help Brady with his things while I fix a pot of coffee."

As George escorted his guest down the hall, Brady commented, "That's quite a lady you've latched onto. I didn't think you had it in you."

"Neither did I," George admitted. "As much as I love to fly, it wouldn't mean a thing without her to come home to."

"Well, Little Wing, count yourself lucky you found her first." Brady's grin didn't quite disarm his insinuation.

"You'd have been out of luck," George countered.

"Oh yeah?"

"Yeah. She's met your kind before."

Brady gave a rueful chuckle. "Maybe you're right."

"How do you mean?"

"I've met her kind before, too."

"So, how long are you in town?" Julia reached across the kitchen table to fill Brady's cup.

"Depends. If all my business goes as planned, I'll be leaving in a couple of days. If not, I could be here a week."

"What sort of business are you in?"

George suppressed a wince at his wife's question, but Brady's reply was perfectly bland: "I work for a large sports equipment manufacturer in Bogota. We're hoping to sign a retail distribution deal with K-Mart, and I'm meeting with the purchasing agent tomorrow to start hammering out the details."

George blinked in amazement. He was no stranger to an occasional embellishment of the truth when it suited his purposes, but the sheer audacity of this lie stunned him. He was also astounded at how plausible it would have sounded, coming from anybody but Brady.

"It sounds very exciting," Julia said. "Business seems to be so international these days."

"Believe me," Brady replied, "it's not nearly as glamorous as it seems. The travel is interesting at first, but too many airports, hotels, restaurants and meetings...well, it takes its toll. I'm ready for a nice Executive VP spot in operations. You know, short days, long lunches, and a membership at the club."

George didn't know what to think, or how to respond to the incredible tapestry Brady was weaving. He decided to let it play out unchallenged. He was curious to see how far Brady would take it.

"That must be tough on your family." To a stranger, Julia's voice would have sounded innocent enough, but to George, it seemed too smooth. He wondered if she really believed all this.

Brady shrugged. "I guess it's fortunate that I've never married."

"Isn't it lonely, going home to an empty house?"

George broke in: "I'm sure Brady is perfectly happy with his life. I know plenty of guys who'd envy him." He caught his wife's challenging glance. The conversation was getting out of hand.

Brady cut across him, smoothly. "Truth is, Julia, I envy your husband." He paused just long enough to communicate just what it was that he envied. "In many ways he has been much more successful than me."

Julia caught the compliment and smiled. Brady's earlier air of nervousness had evaporated, leaving him looking confident and relaxed. He returned her smile.

Later, as she lay beside George in bed, Julia asked, "How long did you know Brady before you lost touch with him?"

George thought for a moment before he answered. "Less than a year, though it seemed like he was my closest friend at the time. It's funny how that happens. When you're young, tradition and roots don't mean as much."

"Mmmm."

"Someone you've just met can seem as important as someone you've known all your life. I guess when your hormones are in high gear, you're more attuned to animal magnetism."

"So, you and Brady—"

George interrupted. "That's not what I meant."

Julia laughed. "What exactly did you mean, then?"

"It's just interesting how someone you hardly know can become such a big factor in your life. Brady had it all going for him...or at least that's how it seemed at the time. The rest of us were still in school, but he actually had a job."

"What did he do?"

"He worked at the Ford Rouge plant, so he had money, a decent car, the best dope. He knew his way around. I really looked up to him. But he could be cruel too, if he was pissed off about something, he'd put you down. It didn't matter who was around or what was going on. There were times when I hated him, when I—" George caught himself. There was no point telling Julia that he'd feared Brady too, sometimes. "When I wished I'd never met him," he concluded lamely.

"Sounds complicated," she said. "How do you feel about him now?"

"At first, I wasn't even sure about inviting him over, but after we got talking, all those memories and emotions began to well up. It was only a few months, but we shared a lot. Maybe it's like soldiers who've been in combat together; they don't really know each other, but the experience is so intense that the bond becomes strong."

In the early hours, listening to his wife's gentle breathing, George considered—not for the first time—the paradox of how the worst part of his life had led to the best part. If it wasn't for his involvement with Brady and the Social Coalition, he would never have met her.

Julia's father owned a large plastics manufacturing business in Detroit, and one of his suppliers was located in Montana. He often flew chartered flights into the airport where George worked. Sometimes he was accompanied by Julia, who was working for her father at the time.

On one of these trips, she'd been hanging around the airport, killing time until her return flight, when she spotted

George pre-flighting the airport's own Piper Navaho. She wandered over to get a closer look at the big twin-engine plane—and, as it turned out, at the pilot who was attending to it. George felt an immediate attraction to the pretty girl with the dark hair and the deep blue eyes. As he answered her questions about the Piper, she made him feel like she was so tuned to him that another plane could have crashed nearby and she wouldn't have noticed. She seemed to have the ability to get past the surface, to reach into a man's soul. It was unnerving at first, but whatever she did was done with such empathy that George soon felt completely at ease.

When she mentioned that her schedule brought her to Montana regularly, George resolved to keep an eye out for her. Several weeks later, he managed to ask her to dinner. The chemistry was obvious. Their different lives meant they couldn't spend much time together, but they could write and call one another frequently—and they did.

Julia's father had offered many times to put George on as a salesman. George was confident that the older man would have been an agreeable boss—they got along well—and it would have meant better money and regular hours and, most importantly, being located in Julia's home town. But he knew he wouldn't last long with his feet on the ground. So Julia's father had hooked him up with Haley, who was looking for a corporate pilot, and at last George was able to move to Detroit. Within a year, he and Julia were married.

As George lay staring at the ceiling, he wondered what would have happened if Julia had been around in those insane days with Brady and the boys. Would she have even noticed him, or would she have been just another Brady Keyes statistic? The troubling thought stayed with him as he drifted off, and seemed to taint his dreams.

Chapter 5

Sunlight danced on the dark blue waves of Lake Michigan, ten thousand feet below. This was the sort of run that made George's job. Much as he loved his work, being at the beck and call of a passenger like Haley could sometimes be demeaning. Things were different when flying alone through crystal skies: George could lose himself completely. He could even imagine that *Haley's Comet* was his, and that he was on his way to seek adventure.

As he pushed on, mesmerized by the droning engines and the beauty of the day, he wondered why he felt so apprehensive about his appointment to dine with Brady Keyes that night. On the surface, it seemed the perfect recipe for a great time: two old friends out for a night on the town and—with Julia visiting her folks for the evening—no hurry to get home. But when Brady had suggested the meeting, there'd been something in his voice that alerted George that Brady had another agenda.

And what about that cock'n'bull story he'd fed Julia? If Brady's business in Detroit were legitimate, George was the CEO of General Motors. He knew that Brady had come to see him, and that it wasn't to renew an old acquaintance. George shrugged. He'd find the truth soon enough. Right now he had a job to do and, on a day like this, a pretty good one.

Six hours later, George strolled into the Gold Room Restaurant in Southfield. He straightened his tie uncomfortably as the oily Maitre d' looked for Brady's reservation. George hated restaurants that required a jacket and tie.

"Ah, yes. Mr. Keyes is already here. Let me show you to his table," said the Maitre d'. Brady was already here? Another red flag went up. Brady had never been known for his punctuality, and George had expected to end up memorizing the menu while he waited for Brady to make his usual dramatic entrance.

As they wove their way among the crowded tables, George noted the glimmer and glamour of the other patrons: silver haired sophisticates; Bloomfield Hills squires dining with their well-dressed wives; starry-eyed beauties hanging on every word of their gray-haired escorts. Then the Maitre d' was leading him toward Brady, who was sipping a drink and unabashedly admiring the female attractions. It was strange to see this former social outlaw sitting amidst all this bourgeois decadence. Brady caught George's eye. "*Que Pasa,* Little Wing?"

"Hi, Brady." George gestured his thanks to the Maitre d', and sat down. "How'd your meeting go today?"

Brady ignored the question. "Can you believe the action in this place? Look at that one." Brady indicated a stunning blonde, two tables away, who was accepting a light from her flawlessly-groomed companion. "Bet you'd forget you're married if that came on to you."

George directed an embarrassed glance at the girl. "She's beautiful," he said, "but it would take more than that to make me forget Julia."

"Come on, man, this is Brady you're talking to. Just because you have a great main course doesn't mean you don't like to sample an hors d'oeuvre now and then, right?"

"It probably seems lame to you," George said carefully,

"but what I have with Julia...well, I wouldn't throw it away on some bimbo."

"That's no bimbo." Brady inclined his head toward the blonde. "That's pure class."

"Whatever. It's just not my style."

"You always were a little backward in that department, Little Wing." Brady grinned. "A few months in Colombia would've cured you of that."

"Well, I'll never find out now. Just as well, I guess."

Brady eyed George warily. He started to say something, but hesitated as the waiter approached. Both men listened as the man recited the specials. Brady ordered beer. With a disapproving sniff and a glance at the wine list, the waiter stalked off to fetch their orders.

"So tell me," Brady began, "how have things been for you? Really?"

Brady's tone seemed sincere, and George was taken aback. "What do you mean? I told you things were going great."

"No, man. We're past the polite bullshit now. I want to know what's really going on."

"It wasn't bullshit, Brady. My life has never been better. I've got a great job, and a wife I hardly deserve. A nice house in a decent neighborhood. And I'm feeling better about myself than I have in twenty years. What else is there to say?"

"Money, for one thing. Are you trying to tell me that a pilot for a small corporation makes enough to support a woman like Julia in the style she deserves?"

George bristled: it was a sore point. "Julia works too."

Brady gave a knowing smile. "As long as that's the way she wants it."

"Julia works because it takes two incomes to turn our nut. That's how it is with most people these days. Anyway, she likes being involved with her father's business. She may end up taking over some day."

"I wasn't trying to offend you, man. I just didn't think you'd fall for that middle-class crap. And I sure didn't think you'd want to depend on your wife to support you in your golden years...playing golf in St. Petersburg, no doubt."

George frowned. "What in the hell are you driving at?"

"I'm just interested in your welfare."

"Bullshit. I know you, Brady. I know you're not here to sell basketballs to K-Mart."

Brady flashed a smile, but it didn't seem to include his eyes; they looked as cold and hard as chips of flint. "You're right. Let's cut the crap and get down to business."

Brady's new demeanor reminded George just how intimidating the man could be. He listened with growing unease as Brady continued, "Do you remember a big drug bust in Detroit two years ago?"

George laughed, trying to keep it light. It would never do to let Brady know just how bothered he was. "Are you kidding? Which one of the 5,000 drug busts that year are you talking about?"

"The one that made national headlines. The one that involved the brother of Carlos Santez."

"The Colombian druglord?"

Brady nodded. "The same."

"Yeah. Now that you mention it, I remember the splash it made. Why?"

"Carlos Santez is a friend of mine. A good friend."

A wave of nausea washed over George . He didn't like where this was going. "Before you say another thing, I'm not interested in your business. Let's just have a nice meal and talk about old times, okay?"

Brady stared at George for a long moment. "You owe it to yourself to hear me out. You owe it to your wife, too."

The waiter arrived with their drinks and stood poised to take their food orders. Feeling far from hungry, George went with an appetizer. Brady ordered a French dish George had never heard of.

"As I was saying," Brady continued once the waiter had left, "Carlos is a friend of mine. And sort of a business partner too."

"I knew it," George sneered.

"You don't know shit, man. Shut up and listen."

George shifted back in his seat, cowed by Brady's whip-crack reply.

Brady continued smoothly, as if nothing had happened. "Santez was a big drug dealer, and I worked with him when he was on his way up. Now he's so damn rich he doesn't know what to do with his money. Lately, the drug trade has gotten a little intense in Colombia. Santez doesn't need the heartburn, so he's turning his attention to other things, even getting involved in legitimate businesses."

"And you?"

"I'm his business partner. Where he goes, I go." Brady smiled slyly. "In fact we have been talking to some businesses in the US about buying some Colombian products. But that's not why I came to Detroit."

"I didn't think so. Go on."

"I'm here to help Carlos tie up a piece of unfinished business. Carlos is a very sentimental man..." George snorted, but Brady just plowed on, "...and family means everything to him. Especially since he lost his father and older brother to the drug wars."

"So?"

"He wants his baby brother back. Hector."

"And what do you want from me?"

"It's not what I want from you, Little Wing, it's what I can do for you." Brady was turning on the charm again, just like George remembered. It was a manipulative trick—a bad cop, good cop routine rolled up into one person. The old power was still there, even now that George understood the technique. He steeled himself, determined to remain unmoved. "Do for me?"

"Listen, I know you like to fly, but do you really like flying for the man?"

"It's a good job."

"Yeah, but how'd you like to have your own business? A going little charter service with a couple of hot planes, maybe even a Lear or a nice Citation?"

Brady was laying it on thick, but George was already tiring of the game. "Sure, who wouldn't? Get to the point."

Brady looked genuinely offended. "I'm only trying to understand your dreams, Little Wing."

Their food arrived. George stared at his plate until the waiter left. "Brady, my dreams are my own business, but the kind of planes it takes to run a decent charter are way out of my reach."

"How about the plane you fly now? And, say, $250,000? Would that be good enough to start a business?" Brady unfolded his napkin. "You help me complete my mission for Carlos, and I'll see to it that you'll have *Haley's Comet,* and the money."

Here it comes, George thought. Whatever the job entailed, the risks had to be astronomical for Brady to offer a reward like that.

Brady leaned forward and lowered his voice conspiratorially. "I happen to know that your boss is a good friend of Albert Strand, the federal judge who convicted Hector. I also happen to know that Haley has invited Judge Strand for a weekend at his fishing lodge in Canada. And I know who is going to fly them there."

George was incredulous. "How'd you find out about that?"

"Carlos Santez told me. You wouldn't believe the ways he has of getting information." Brady speared a sautéed potato on his fork. "I even know how much Judge Strand lost to Haley during their last golf match."

"Why are you telling me this? Do you expect me to get involved in some scheme to extort an early release for Hector Santez? If you are, I'll save you some time. The answer is no."

"Hear me out, Little Wing. All you have do is divert that flight to an alternate landing strip and turn your back while Haley and the Judge are escorted to a detaining facility. I guarantee you that no harm will come to either one. And you fly away with a million-dollar airplane."

If this had come from anybody else, George would have simply stood up and left. With Brady, that wasn't an option: there was no telling how the man might respond. George decided to humor him. "Supposing I was stupid enough to go along with this so-called plan. Where do you suppose I could fly the plane to? Don't you think the authorities in the US and Canada might be looking for it?"

"That's why you'd be operating your new business in Colombia."

George laughed. "You've got me pegged, don't you?. That's just what I've been thinking about doing—giving up everything I've worked for, leaving my wife, leaving the States, all so I can fly a stolen plane in some banana republic while I look over my shoulder for the DEA, CIA, FBI, and who knows who else. Yep, you got it, pal."

Brady's jaw tightened. "Julia would go with you. And you wouldn't be moving into a hostile environment. You'd be under Carlos Santez's protection, and Santez runs Colombia. Come on, I've seen how you live. Carlos takes care of his friends. How could you lose?"

"Drug lords have a habit of going down from time to time. Anyway, even if I went along with this, what makes you think Julia would?"

"I've seen you together. She'd follow you."

George shrugged. "Thanks, but no thanks."

Brady looked as surprised as George felt. They were both in unfamiliar territory: in the old days, Brady would have bullied George into going along with whatever the latest harebrained scheme happened to be. Now, he said nothing, but his lip curled into a sneer and his body coiled like a spring.

George made his tone conciliatory. "Come on, Brady. No offense. Let's just enjoy our meal and let it go at that, okay?"

Brady leaned forward, his voice a hiss. "You misunderstand me if you imagine I'd return to Carlos Santez with the news that I failed to retrieve his brother because I couldn't secure the services of the pilot."

George felt the hair prickling on the back of his neck. He said nothing.

"I hate to insist, but given your narrow-minded attitude, I have no alternative. And neither do you."

The chill was like standing in front of an open freezer. George tried to hide his fear, but he couldn't help blinking under Brady's cold gaze. "What's that suppose to mean?"

"It means you have a nice life. And a nice wife. You don't need me to spell it out."

"If anything happens to Julia—"

"You can't protect her. Not from these people. And something tells me you won't be running to the police for help, either."

George had seen that one coming: it was the one hold Brady had over him. Brady wouldn't hesitate to notify the authorities of George's involvement with the bungled art heist. Then George would go to prison, or back into hiding—back to a life that held no home, no Julia, no flying.

"You should close your mouth, Little Wing," Brady said with a sneer. "You look like a fish."

The surge of hatred that George felt was so strong that it left a taste like metal on his tongue. "Doesn't honor mean anything to you? We were all in it together. Steve, Pete, Bobby, you and me."

Brady shrugged. "Honor is for people who have choices. Santez is a generous friend, but he can be disagreeable to those who…test the limits of his friendship."

George pushed his plate away. "Why did you screw around with all this K-Mart bullshit, Brady? Why didn't you just lay it out the moment we met back at the airport? You knew it would come to this."

"I thought that if I presented it in the right way, you might listen to reason."

"You're full of shit. You knew I'd never go for a scheme like this, unless I was forced to."

"Well, that's the question, isn't it? Cooperation comes before coercion in my dictionary. But if cooperation doesn't do the job, I move on to the next step."

George thought about all he stood to lose. Twenty years of rebuilding his life. Establishing roots and gaining respect in a community. It was a community he'd once ridiculed, but he still valued the niche he had carved out.

Now, all of it was about to unravel because of a man who had come briefly into his life, more than two decades ago.

And then there was Julia. Even if he sometimes took her

for granted, she was his lifeline. She was the one who'd helped him gain his self-respect, encouraged him to push beyond his limits and build a life that was fulfilling. As much as he loved flying, it was coming home to Julia that really mattered. If he were to lose her, life would be meaningless.

Brady was still waiting for a response, a slight smile on his face. Suddenly, George understood. Once, he'd been awed by this cruel man. He'd admired Brady's determination and self-belief, the man's relentless ability to dominate any situation. The fact that George himself lacked these qualities made them seem all the more admirable.

Now, he despised Brady—but that iron will was still there. Brady wouldn't hesitate to destroy everything that George loved. Twenty years had passed, but the balance of power between them hadn't changed one bit.

"Tell me what you want me to do."

"It's too bad it had to be like this, Little Wing. This would have been fun, back in the old days."

"Well, it's not the old days. This is my life you're fucking with, so let's just get it over with."

Brady crumpled his napkin and motioned to the waiter to bring them their bill. "Let's get out of here. I want you to meet the rest of the players and show you what you need to know."

Chapter 6

A rain shower had passed over while they were in the restaurant, its presence betrayed by the dark sheen on the parking lot, now emanating gentle wisps of steam into the warm spring evening. George stood silently next to Brady while the valet boys sprinted off to retrieve their cars. The anger that gripped him was tempered by a strange sense of loss. As difficult as his relationship with Brady had been, he had thought of him as a friend. Now he saw the man who stood next to him as a stranger who had betrayed him.

And worse than any personal betrayal: the man had threatened Julia.

George stared straight ahead. There was nothing to say. The silence added to the dreamlike quality of his state of mind. Had they really only spent an hour in the restaurant? It felt more like a week. His life with Julia was the real dream. Standing here in the humid night with Brady, waiting for the cars to arrive—that was the nightmare.

Brady's rented Cadillac pulled up, George's worn Ford Taurus right behind. Brady's voice sounded far away. "Follow me. Here's my cellphone number, in case you get lost." He handed George a slip of paper as he stepped off the curb toward his car.

As they wove their way through the dark Southfield streets, the glow of the Cadillac's taillights reflected off the black, shining pavement. George kept pace, although it wasn't easy.

Brady wasn't even trying to make sure that George would make the lights, or manage to follow around slower traffic.

As they pulled into the parking lot of the Holiday Inn on Telegraph, George fought off the panic that was settling in. He tried to focus. He had to concentrate, to be alert to every detail, every nuance. He pulled into a parking space a few cars down from the Cadillac, got out, and headed for the lobby. Brady strode silently a few paces ahead. At the entrance, he waited for George to catch up, and they went through the crowded reception area together. As if in answer to George's silent plea, several people were waiting at the elevator door. They all jostled inside when the doors opened.

Brady led the way out of the elevator at the fourth floor. Silently, the men made their way down the corridor to room 415. Brady knocked while George leaned against the wall. The faint sound of a TV inside the room was suddenly shut off, its place taken by muffled voices and movement from inside. The door opened a crack. At first, all George could see was an eye peering out, then the door opened fully, revealing a tall, muscular, well-dressed black man who motioned them inside.

"You're early," he said to Brady. George had been expecting a Colombian, but the black man's voice held no trace of a Spanish accent.

"It's called efficient, Roy." Brady pushed past the man and into the living room of a large suite. George followed, barely glancing at Roy, though aware of the man's intense stare. Brady motioned for George to take one of the four seats arranged around a table in the middle of the room. The rest of the furniture had been pushed to the walls. Seated at the table were two young men, Latino by their appearance, and well-dressed. Roy took the fourth seat, across from George, while Brady leaned on the dressing table and lit a cigarette.

"I suppose some introductions are in order. You met Roy Lassiter already." He indicated the black man who had answered the door. Lassiter was middle-aged and handsome. He stifled a smirk. Brady gestured to George's right. "Juan Gutierrez and Tony Lopez." Gutierrez had slicked-back, curly hair and fine features, almost baby-faced. Lopez was in his late twenties, with straight black hair, also slicked back, and features that revealed his Indian heritage.

George couldn't resist. "You gentlemen with K-Mart?"

"So cynical, Little Wing," answered Brady before anyone else could react. "These are my business associates."

George studied the men around the table. The two Latinos smiled dumbly. He wondered if they understood English. Lassiter still looked amused.

"Roy here is our associate in Detroit. He handles all of the liaison with our local business partners. Juan and Tony are Carlos's cousins. They often accompany me on my business trips to assure everything goes smoothly."

"A regular Boy Scout troop, I'm sure."

"Don't get cute with my friends here," Brady snapped. "They think I'm being far too patient with you as it is. If it were up to them, you'd have been doing whatever they wanted, five minutes after they met you."

Lassiter's smirk had been replaced by a cold dead stare. The two Latinos were glaring, too. George decided that Brady was telling the truth. "I just want to get this over with as quickly as possible. Can we get down to business?"

Brady approached the table. "Roy, would you show him where we're going?"

Lassiter reached behind his chair and produced a map, which he spread out in front of George. It depicted all of Michigan and most of Ontario, Canada. A large red circle had been drawn around Lake Eabamet in Northern Ontario. Inside the circle, an 'X' was marked at the southeastern end of the lake. He instantly recognized it as the location of Haley's fishing camp. George and Haley had flown there many times. It was breathtakingly beautiful, and starkly remote.

Fifteen miles across the lake to the northeast was Fort Hope, an Indian Reserve of about eight hundred people. George had spent many hours at the Fort Hope Airstrip, waiting for Haley's boat to cross the lake for the return journey. He had never seen the camp itself, except from the air.

"I see you know the territory," Brady said. "That will save

us some time. Haley plans to leave next Friday morning, and he will be allowed to do so."

George knew of Haley's plans already, of course, but he held his peace. Brady continued, "He means to return from the camp on Sunday evening—however this will not be the case. He and Judge Strand will never even arrive there. They will be our guests near Ogoki Lake, right here." Brady jabbed a finger at another 'X' on the map, about fifty miles south and east of the camp. He looked at George. "Your job will be to bring Haley and Strand to this location rather than the fishing camp."

"And just how do you propose I do that?"

"Very simple. While you're en route, you'll declare an emergency and put down right were you are, which will just happen to be right over Ogoki Lake."

"Haley's not stupid. He knows there there's not much that can force a plane down immediately."

"There is one thing that would be both plausible and—"

George finished the sentence. "Fire."

Brady grinned. "Still sharp as a razor, aren't you?"

"And just how do I convince Haley that there is a fire on board?"

"We will give you a remote-controlled smoke device," Lassiter said. "You'll plant it inside one of the engine nacelles."

Brady smiled. "Believe me, once you trigger this thing, your passengers will be looking for their parachutes." Lassiter let out a snicker.

"Seriously," Brady continued, "when you declare the emergency, they're only going to be concerned with the plane getting down safely."

George groped for another objection. "*Haley's Comet* isn't fitted with pontoons."

"That's why you'll be using the airstrip. It's close to the camp we'll be visiting." Brady handed him an aerial photograph of Ogoki Lake. There was a small cluster of buildings. About a quarter of a mile south, George could make out a grass strip and a two-track leading to the camp. Although the strip appeared just big enough to accommodate *Haley's Comet,* it was completely surrounded by a dense pine forest. Losing power on approach or attempting a go-around would be hairy indeed.

"What if Haley and Strand figure out something is fishy? What then?"

"You'll be on the ground before they have any idea that anything's going on. After that, my people will handle everything."

George was reminded of a similar scene from twenty years ago. Plans like these always sounded easy when it was just a bunch of guys sitting around a hotel room, but he knew from bitter experience just how wrong a seemingly buttoned-down plan could go when it came up against the real world.

He imagined the look on Haley's face when he discovered the betrayal. It made George feel sick. Haley believed in him. Haley had given him the opportunity to get his life back on track. Haley had handed the command of a million dollar airplane to a relatively low-time commercial pilot—an act of trust that was inspiring, and that George was expected to destroy. How could he?

Panic threatened to overwhelm him. His heart was hammering. He had to say something. "Brady, we both know there's no such thing as a foolproof plan. There's always some unexpected hitch. I'm trying to anticipate as much as I can. I want to cover every angle."

"I admire your diligence," Brady said. "You are an example to us all."

Lassiter guffawed.

Brady continued, "After you drop off Haley and Strand, the rest is easy. You return to Detroit with 'orders' from Haley to make a run to Texas for some parts. You gather up as much of your stuff as you can—including your loving wife—and then you disappear. Since it will be a weekend, no one should think it's strange that you're gone a couple of days. That will buy you some time. Then you take off for Colombia. You make fuel stops at designated airports along the way, which are operated by our friends, and by the time the authorities have any idea what's going on, you'll be under Carlos' protection, ready to start a new—and I must say—more exciting life."

"Exciting? Try 'ruined'. Try 'blackmailed'." George regretted the words as soon as they were out of his mouth. He glanced at Tony and Juan. They stared back impassively.

"Skip the dramatics," Brady said. "We've been through that. All I want is your assurance that our little adventure will proceed as planned."

"What choice do I have?"

"Several, all but one of which would be exceedingly detrimental to your well-being."

George shrugged. "You've got me by the balls. I'll follow the plan. Just don't think I'm doing it as a 'favor for an old friend'"

"Fine. Go home and start thinking about how much you're going to enjoy your career change. Don't do anything out of the ordinary. Just proceed as normal until D-day."

George got up and glanced around the room. He felt as though he was being released from jail after making bail—but the sense of freedom was tempered by the dread of a trial that could only end in a guilty verdict. "What if something comes up that might jeopardize the plan? How should I get in touch with you?"

Brady scribbled on a Holiday Inn notepad. "Just call this number and say it's 'Little Wing' and hang up. Someone will get in touch."

George folded the paper, put it in his wallet and headed toward the door. "It's been a little slice of heaven, Brady." He nodded at Lassiter and the two Colombians. "See you boys around. I bet we're all going to be real chummy down in Colombia."

Chapter 7

The weather had turned wet again as George left the hotel. He ran for his car, already shivering from the rain—and not only from the rain. In the vehicle, he turned on the defroster. The cool airflow made his shivering worse. He turned up the heat. By the time he pulled onto Telegraph Road, the inside of the car was tropically humid.

He tried to make sense of the last few hours. There had to be a way out of this mess. Julia would never go for it. She'd insist that he turn the matter over to the police, and wherever the chips fell—that's where they'd fall.

It wasn't just Julia. George had to do the right thing for his own reasons, too. If it were just a matter of facing jail time for a twenty year-old crime, he might agree, but Brady had made it clear that there was more at stake than that. And George knew Brady well enough to be certain it wasn't an idle threat.

How could he persuade Julia that these people were dangerous?

The rain came down harder as he wound his way through Rochester and into his own neighborhood. Occasional lightning flashes illuminated the newly leafed trees. Most of the houses were dark, but he caught glimpses of televisions flickering through windows. Once or twice he saw neighbors watching him drive by as they peered out at the storm.

It was almost 1:00 a.m. when he pulled into the driveway, next to Julia's car. He went into the house. All was dark except for the tropical fish tank, which bubbled in a purple glow as the colorful creatures flitted back and forth. He watched them as the lightning flashed through the curtains, distorting the images weirdly. Julia would be asleep by now. He tip-toed to the living room couch and sat down.

Everything was familiar, but he viewed the place with a strange detachment, as though it belonged to someone else, while he was no more than a guest who'd overstayed his welcome. He felt as though the past twenty years had been lived on borrowed time.

A stack of flying magazines sat on the table, waiting until he had time to read them. They represented the career that he loved, and that was now becoming his undoing. He buried his face in his hands. Was this the long-postponed punishment that he deserved?

An incessant ringing nagged its way into his consciousness. He recognized the noise as the telephone. He must have fallen asleep on the couch. The luminous face of his watch told him it was 3:30 a.m.

Julia was a light sleeper: why hadn't she answered the phone next to her bed?

The ringing continued. With some effort, he pulled himself up and staggered to the extension in his den. He picked up the handset and croaked, "Hello?"

The line was silent for a few seconds. "I see you haven't gone to bed yet, Little Wing, otherwise you'd have called me. Are you sitting down?"

"What the hell do you want? I said I'd do it. Can't I even get a night's sleep?"

"You're not going to like this," Brady said. "You'd better sit down."

"You've screwed me around enough for one evening. Nothing you could possibly tell me would—"

Brady cut across him. "Julia won't be coming home tonight."

George dropped the phone and raced to the bedroom. He turned on the light and saw the silent testimony of the perfectly-made bed. It had obviously not been slept in. He fought back the fear and anger that were welling up inside of him, and snatched up the phone next to the bed. "Where the hell is my wife?"

"She'll be at the rendezvous point when you drop off Haley and Strand."

This had to be a joke. Brady was going to laugh uproariously in a moment, and Julia would come out from wherever she was hiding...but deep down, George knew he'd heard the truth. "Where is she?"

"She's safe. Nobody will touch her, as long as you cooperate. That's all you need to know."

"I want to talk to her."

"You will."

"I mean now, you asshole!"

"She's not available at the moment. One of our female associates is taking care of her, so you needn't worry about her wellbeing."

"When can I talk to her?"

"In a few minutes. She'll call you back. You'll have sixty seconds to establish that it is Julia and that she is okay." Brady paused. "Not entirely happy, but okay."

"Why?" George demanded. "Why'd you screw with me at dinner? Why didn't you just drop the hammer and get it over with?"

"Honestly, I didn't decide to involve Julia directly until after we left the restaurant. I was hoping you'd be reasonable, but your attitude made me...uncomfortable. This is too important for me to take risks."

"I told you I'd cooperate."

"And I believed that you would," Brady said. "Now I'm certain of it."

George closed his eyes. He couldn't think. He could hardly breathe. Was his heart still beating? Everything looked dim, like flying in haze with no clear horizon. With superhuman effort, he pulled out of the graveyard spiral of grief and fear, saved by another emotion: rage. "If anything happens to Julia, you'll have more to fear from me than you ever would from Carlos Santez."

"George, hang up and wait for Julia's call."

The line went dead. George sat with the handset to his ear for several seconds, then replaced it in the cradle. He gazed around the room and saw a framed photograph taken of himself and Julia on a rare vacation in San Diego. He saw Julia's jewelry box, her brush and hand mirror, her perfume bottles. The curtains she'd chosen. The furniture she loved. The vase of spring flowers she kept next to the bed.

Everything spoke of her: the room was shaped by her personality, not his. But he loved it that way. Julia gave shape and meaning to his life, too. His limbs felt numb as he trudged back down to the den and replaced the receiver there.

Almost immediately, the phone trilled. Only a few seconds seemed to have passed, but the clock on his desk told him it was almost twenty minutes since Brady's call. He reached over and picked up. "Julia?"

"George Ashton?" asked a male voice.

"Yeah. Who is this?"

The voice on the other end was speaking to someone away from the phone. "Put the woman on."

The line clicked as another extension was picked up. "Hello? Who's there?" It was Julia. She sounded frightened.

"Julia? It's me, George."

"George! George...what the hell is going on? Where are you?"

George fought to keep his voice calm. "Are you all right, honey?"

"No, I'm not all right. I'm being held against my will by crazy people. They won't tell me anything. What is going on?"

"Has anyone hurt you."

"Yes...well no, not exactly. They grabbed me in the driveway. Then they blindfolded and gagged me and shoved me into a car. They've brought me into this disgusting house... George, it's horrible!"

George's heart ached at the thought of Julia being manhandled by Lassiter's people, but he tried to reassure her. "Look, Julia, they're not going to hurt you. They just want something from me and they are using you to make sure they get it."

"Why, George, Why?"

"Julia, we don't have much time, I'll tell you all about it when I see you. Just do as they say and they won't hurt you."

The voice came on the other phone, "That's it, boys and girls, time to say goodnight."

George needed more. "Wait, just a few more seconds—"

The line went dead. He slammed the handset down and swore at it.

Julia stood by the phone, quietly sobbing. Two large hands came down on her shoulders, gentle but firm and strong. "Take it easy, honey. Ain't nothing gonna happen to you. We're just keeping an eye on you for a few days."

Julia shrugged the hands away and turned to face the tall, brown woman behind her. "Who's doing this? What do they want from George?"

"I can't tell you. They don't tell me nothing. I'm just supposed to make sure you're okay and that you don't try to go nowhere."

"Well, I'm not okay as long as I'm here." Julia looked around her prison: a small basement bedroom, untouched for many years. The sheet-rock walls were clean, but the paint was faded and cracked. Unfilled nail holes gave testimony to the many pictures that must have been hung by previous residents. There were no windows. The floor was covered by tile that, judging from the pattern, dated from the fifties. The dropped ceiling was crisscrossed with the metal framework that held the cork tiles, and the fluorescent lighting rounded out the picture of a weekend handyman's dismal efforts to add value to his home.

"Why are you doing this to me?"

"I told you, I just do what I'm told, and so should you. It'll make this a lot easier on both of us."

Julia forced herself to calm down. Any information she could obtain might help her somehow. The best thing would be to keep the woman talking. "What's your name?"

"You can call me Naomi."

"So what's in this for you?"

"I get to keep my job."

"What's that? Your job, I mean."

"Ain't we the curious one? I don't see that it makes any difference to you."

Julia shrugged. "I just figured that if we're going to be spending some time together, it might be nice to know a little about each other."

"I know all I need to know about you," Naomi said. "You're a rich little girl from the suburbs, who's got her little white ass in a sling and would probably shoot me dead in the blink of an eye if she could get her hands on a gun."

"Whatever gave you the idea that I was rich?"

"Sure you're rich. Why else would Roy Lassiter and his Colombian buddy—" Naomi clammed up, as if she'd already said more than she should.

Julia pounced on the mistake. "So this has something to do with Colombians."

Naomi stared at her. "You wanna get through this?"

Julia nodded.

"Then you better do what I tell you, and right now I'm telling you to keep your nose out of what don't concern you." The big woman grabbed Julia by the elbow and marched her to a small, stained sofa on the other side of the room. "Now sit." A meaty shove backed up the order. Once Julia was on the couch, Naomi handed her a ripped wool blanket and told her, "Get some sleep. You're gonna need it."

Chapter 8

Something was burning George's eyelids. Squinting, he sat up and saw that the glare was a slanting bar of sunlight reflecting off the mirror over Julia's dresser, and onto the bedspread where his head had lain.

The curtains were undrawn and he was still fully dressed. He'd slept on the coverlet. He eased himself into a sitting position and groaned. It had been a rough night. He pressed his knuckles to his eyes, as if to erase the memory of the previous evening—the dinner with Brady, the threats, the hotel room.

Julia gone. His life gone.

He lowered his hands and opened his eyes. The beveled edge of the mirror cast a slender rainbow on the wall. His life was like that, broken into pieces on Highway 89. He'd spent the last twenty years trying to make something whole from the fragments.

He might as well have tried to mend a broken rainbow.

The night before, he'd have done anything to get out of betraying Haley and the Judge, but Brady had anticipated his reaction and kidnapped Julia. There could have been no more effective way to ensure George's cooperation.

Brady had always been ruthless. He had never hesitated to lie, cajole, dominate and manipulate to get what he wanted. With a cleverness matched only by his greed, the man practiced amorality as if it were an art form. And I admired him, George thought. Because he is everything I am not.

He rose on unsteady legs and lurched into the bathroom. His reflection shocked him—hair sticking out in all directions, eyes bloodshot and puffy, a dense, scratchy shadow of morning beard. If he hadn't known better, he'd have sworn he was just coming off a two-day bender. He had to pull himself together, he had to be normal. He showered, shaved and groomed away most of the damage. Back in the bedroom, he pulled on his weekend Levi's, the T-shirt he'd picked up at the 1988 Oshkosh Airshow, with its barely visible P-51 Mustang, and his running shoes.

Twenty minutes later, he was sipping instant coffee and gnawing on a stale Danish while gazing out the dining room window at his neighbor, Phil Lukich. Phil was pushing his Toro back and forth across his front lawn.

Once, George would have laughed at Phil's endless routine—chained to his desk at Chevrolet all week, chores around the house on Saturday, Church on Sunday morning and dinner afterwards with the in-laws in Saint Clair Shores. Now, watching his neighbor guiding the mower with nothing worse to look forward to than a cold beer and a TV ballgame, George decided that suburban predictability had never looked more appealing.

He went into the den and sat at his desk. As usual, it was disorganized and messy—bills he had to pay, junk mail branded with coffee cup rings piled in one corner, letters he should answer or file away, and a stack of magazines and books he'd been meaning to read. He wondered how bad his den would have been, without Julia's tidying hand.

George decided to attack the problem as he had done so often in the past. Pushing the largest pile of paper aside, he reached for a pad of yellow legal paper and a pen, and tried to describe the situation in writing.

Ten minutes later, he was still idly drumming with the pen and staring out at Phil, who was now working on the backyard while surreptitiously peering at his next-door neighbor sunning herself by her pool. George tossed the pen aside and decided to go for a walk.

He returned after an hour and sat on his front porch, sweaty, confused and frustrated. Phil was now sweeping grass clippings off the sidewalk. He looked up for a moment and spotted George. "Hey, neighbor!" he shouted. "Done with your chores already?" He strolled toward George.

Shit. The last thing George needed was small talk with Phil Lukich. Maybe he could head him off. He nodded at the unswept clippings. "Shouldn't you finish clearing up before you start goofing off? I don't want Melissa on my case for contributing to your delinquency."

Phil was just a few steps away. "I put my time in today. How about a couple of beers? You look like you could use one as much as me."

There was no way to get out of this now. "I guess I'm supposed to buy?"

"Of course, good buddy. You don't want me to deplete my stocks, do you?" Phil's beer mooching was notorious around the neighborhood.

George got up and led the way into the house. "From what I hear, you've still got the first six-pack you bought after moving into that house. Come on, you scumbag."

In the kitchen, he grabbed a dish towel and wiped sweat off his face and neck while Phil grabbed two beers from the fridge. "Man, I gotta get one of the neighborhood kids to do that lawn for me. I'm getting too old."

"Maybe you could trade those beer stocks of yours for a lawn service."

Phil snorted. "Melissa would call that 'frivolous expenditure'. If you see a lawn service truck parked outside my house, the next thing you'll see is a police car carting Melissa off for murdering me."

In spite of himself, George smiled. "Does that mean I'd get back all the stuff you've borrowed over the years?"

"What are you talking about? Ain't my fault if you use my house for a land fill to dump all your junk." Phil looked around. "Say, where's Julia? I thought maybe we could get together for a barbecue or something tonight."

George had a story ready, but he still needed a moment to compose himself. He pulled out a chair and sat at the table. "She had some vacation time to use, so she's spending the week with her folks, now that her dad's retired. I couldn't get off, so she went on her own."

"How'd she get there? Isn't that her car parked in the driveway?"

George silently cursed his neighbor's prying. "Her car needs some work, and I told her I'd take it in this week. Her dad picked her up."

Now he'd have to do something with the car.

His neighbor grinned. "A whole week, eh buddy? You got any plans ol' Phil should know about?"

"Is that all you think about? I'll be flying my ass off all week, so what little time I have to myself will be sleeping. Alone," he added before Phil could say anything.

"Damn, you do lead a Spartan existence. If Melissa ever took off with the kids for a week, they'd have to check me into the hospital when they got back."

"Yeah, well, not my style." George wished Phil would just leave, but at least the small talk was distracting him, and helping control his anxiety. Besides, now he had an explanation for Julia's absence. Phil could be relied on to circulate the story around the neighborhood within hours.

Phil drained his beer can. "How about another brewski?"

"Hey, I'd like to, Phil, but I've got to run some errands."

"Come on, pal. With the ol' lady gone, you can do what you want."

George scrambled for a reason. "I've got to get to the bank. Got to get some money in before my checks start bouncing back to me."

"Now, there's something I can relate to. If I had to slice my paycheck any thinner, I'd need a scalpel. Mind if I take one for the road?"

"Help yourself." George watched as Phil pulled a beer out of the refrigerator before he got the words out. "Sorry about the barbecue. Maybe in a couple of weeks, okay?"

"Whatever. Just give us a yell." Phil went to the door.

"Enjoy the beer."

"You bet," Phil replied as he pulled the kitchen door closed behind him.

Chapter 9

Monday dragged by: one long, twenty-four hour test of George's nerves and self-control. He struggled to keep his mind focused on work, and didn't always manage it. His concentration kept lapsing, so that his boss sometimes had to repeat himself two or three times.

"Are you feeling okay?" Haley asked eventually.

George assured him that he was just preoccupied with an upcoming flight review.

By Tuesday morning, George was almost ready to go to the police, but when he showed up at the airport there was a package waiting for him on the desk in the small hanger office. No one had seen who had delivered it.

He closed the door and sat down to open the package. Carefully, he cut off the plain paper wrapping and slit open the taped top. It was full of foam pellets, surrounding something bulky. A typewritten note had been slipped in, next to the packing:

```
Attach this to the inside of one of the
engine nacelles. Place it at least five
inches from the engine itself. The remote
device is pre-tuned to the appropriate
frequency. To activate the device, switch
the remote on and press the red button.
```

George delved among the pellets and pulled out two plastic bags. One held a rectangular-shaped, black plastic box, about the size of two packs of cigarettes placed end to end. On one side of the box was a thick, self-adhesive pad covered with silver backed paper. The second bag held the remote, which was about the size of a pager, with an on/off switch and a circular, red button. George inspected each device, turning them over in his hands.

So this was it.

Suddenly, he knew what he had to do. Luckily, he had no reason to see Haley for the rest of the day and the time slid by in a blur, taken up with maintenance concerns and updating charts. George studied the aerial photos Brady had given him, and pinpointed the area on the charts. He then determined the exact waypoint at which he would activate the smoke device.

He left the airport early, grateful for the sense of relief that comes with confronting a problem head on.

Hints of yellow and red were chasing the darkness from the eastern sky as George steered his car around the on-ramp connecting I75 to eastbound I94. Straightening out, he floored it and prayed for an opening as he tried to merge with the Friday-morning river of oncoming headlights. As usual, he cursed the engineers who'd made the merge lane impossibly short, and winced as some harried driver yielded to his accelerating Ford. Once in the traffic flow, he jockeyed his way past a slowly moving garbage truck. As soon as he passed the Van Dyke exit, he drifted into the right lane to get off on Gratiot.

Several minutes later, he pulled into the parking area at Detroit City Airport. He found a parking spot near the hanger that housed *Haley's Comet*. Clutching his flight bag and map case, he made his way to a side door that opened into the small office area of the hanger.

Ed Scripps, still on duty from the night before, brushed past George as he was heading out the door on his rounds.

"Hi, George."

"'Morning, Ed."

"Got an early flight today, eh?"

George didn't feel like making small talk, but Ed would certainly think it was strange if he was brusque. "Yeah, Mr. Haley wants to get started on a long weekend. He here yet?"

"Haven't seen him. Where are you going?"

"He's got a fishing camp in Canada. He's taking a friend up there." George could hardly believe that he'd actually beaten Haley to the hanger before an early morning flight. But then he hadn't slept much the night before. He'd figured he might as well arrive early, and burn off nervous energy pre-flighting the plane.

"You staying with them?" Ed asked.

"No such luck. Got to get back here for a flight to Houston on Saturday." George broke eye contact, anxious to get to the plane. "Well, I need to get a weather briefing and file a flight plan, so I'd better get moving. Mr. Haley wants to be airborne by 5:30."

"Yeah. Have a nice flight."

"See you later, Ed."

George went into the hanger office and opened his flight bag to retrieve the smoke device and the remote. Once they were secreted in his jacket pocket, he picked up the bag and went out to the flight line. *Haley's Comet* sat on the tarmac next to a fueling truck from Hanson's FBO, Haley's usual source. The fueler was standing on a step ladder at the leading edge of the starboard wing, the large, black hose draped over his shoulder, pumping Jet A into the tank.

George circled the plane, ostensibly preflighting it. He stopped in front of the port engine nacelle. The nose of the plane blocked his view of the man on the ladder. He looked around and, seeing no one else, pulled out the black plastic rectangle, peeled back the silver paper covering the adhesive, and reaching inside the front of the nacelle. The device stuck firmly against the metal. George backed away, glancing past the nose of the plane. The man on the ladder still seemed absorbed in his task.

Satisfied no one had seen him, George moved around the

wing to the door in the aft section, and up the three steps into the passenger compartment. Traversing the short aisle between the eight seats, he caught brief glimpses of the fuel jockey through the passenger windows.

As he reached the cockpit, the man had finished and was working his way down the step ladder, carefully easing the heavy hose down with him. The hose snagged on the top of the ladder and the man looked up to work it free. For an instant, George could see him clearly: a muscular-looking black man, about 30 to 35 years of age, with short hair neatly parted along the left side. The fueler looked over at the cockpit window briefly and saw George looking down at him.

George couldn't remember if he'd ever seen the man before, but he could have sworn he saw the faintest smile creep across the fueler's face before he went back to the truck to begin reeling up the hose.

George took the things he'd need for the flight out of his bag and arranged them strategically in the cockpit. He stowed the bag behind the left seat. Then he went back to the office to finish his flight plan and to file it with the Lansing Flight Service Station.

"Did I oversleep, or did you stay here overnight, George?"

George looked up, startled. He'd been concentrating so intently on the Ontario chart that he hadn't noticed Haley and Judge Strand coming in.

"Sorry, sir. Didn't see you there. No, you didn't oversleep, it's just been a while since I've made this run, so I got here early to spend a little extra time preparing our flight plan."

"George is the best pilot I've ever had, Al," Haley said to Strand. "Not always on time, but he knows how to fly."

"That's all I care about, Jack," answered Strand, as he approached George to shake his hand. "Al Strand, George."

George stood up to meet him. "Nice to meet you, Judge."

Strand was older than Haley, slightly taller, but not nearly as fit. His gray, wavy hair was thinning on top, and a pair of horned-rim glasses sat on his long, aquiline nose, which complemented the sharp, hawk-like features of his face.

As he released George's hand from his firm, practiced politician grip, he said, "Everybody calls me Al."

Knowing that in about two hours, Strand would probably hate him, George did not want to get personal, but he was aware that Haley was watching the interaction. He didn't want to appear uneasy. "Okay, Al." Then, turning to Haley, "Where's your gear?"

"Freddie pulled the car around to the front. He's loading the luggage into the plane right know."

Freddie was Haley's live-in gardener/handyman, who occasionally doubled as chauffeur, especially when Haley wanted to impress one of his passengers.

"Anything special I should be aware of?" George asked, thinking about weight.

"Not really. Just a couple of bags each. All the fishing equipment we'll need is already there. How's the weather looking?"

"Should be a smooth flight."

"No, I mean for the weekend. Are we going to get rained out or anything?"

"A cold front might pass through on Saturday or Sunday... might be a little rain from it on Saturday night or Sunday, but other than that, should be mostly sunny."

"Sounds great, eh Al?" Haley nudged Strand, who smiled lamely. "Come on. Let's get a cup of coffee and let George finish so we can get going."

Haley led the way out of the office and down the hall toward the coffee machine. George sat back down and stared at the charts. It was bad enough that in just two short hours, 'Al'—whom he barely knew—was going to think very poorly of him, but Haley, well that was another story. How could he ever go through with it?

He'd just have to keep thinking of Julia. It was the only thing stronger than his desire to tell Haley everything and get the police involved, and take his chances with his past.

The sun was shining directly in George's eyes as he waited for clearance to turn onto runway 33 for take-off. He glanced over his shoulder and saw Haley and Strand, each clutching a beer can. The two men were talking and laughing, already celebrating the coming weekend of fun and relaxation.

Word came from the tower: "King Air 0418 Sierra, proceed onto runway 33 and hold."

George answered, pushed the throttles forward enough to gain some momentum, turned onto the runway, and pulled the throttles back to idle. He gently braked the plane to a standstill. At least it got the sun out of his eyes. As he waited, he performed last minute checks of the engine gauges and listened intently to the two turboprops for any sign of abnormality.

At last it came. "0418 Sierra, cleared for takeoff. Maintain runway heading until cleared on course."

George smoothly advanced the throttles. The turbine engines whined loudly. Pressed into their seats by the airplane's acceleration, Haley and Strand stopped talking and looked out the windows.

When he reached rotation speed, George gently pulled back on the control wheel and the ground fell away. Feeling slightly superior as he looked down at the bumper to bumper traffic on Van Dyke a few hundred feet below, he maintained a steady climb and waited for instructions from tower to come to course 355.

Julia couldn't open her eyes. Her tongue felt as though it were made out of cotton; it was almost impossible to swallow. It took all her strength to move her hands far enough to pull her eyelids open. For several minutes, she lay staring up at the ceiling, trying to figure out why it looked so strange. Then it hit her—the ceiling was made out of knotty pine, not the suspended tiled affair she had been living under for the past week.

Slowly, she looked around the room. This was definitely not the basement prison. The knotty pine ceiling blended into knotty pine walls, which were adorned with pictures of fish and other wild game. On the wall opposite her, several hideous masks of painted coconut returned her gaze with a blank, unsettling stare. Two large windows brought in dappled sunlight, filtered through towering white pines.

She became aware of a strange noise. Turning her head painfully in the general direction of the sound, she made out Naomi's profile in the bed next to hers. The big woman's mouth was slightly open, and she was snoring gently.

Julia tried to remember where she was and how she'd got here. The last thing she could recall was eating a terrible, fast-food hamburger for lunch. And watching Oprah on a tiny, black and white set. The only way to get a picture at all had been to constantly fiddle with the set's rabbit ears. She remembered lying back on the bed, propping up her head so she could see the television and…nothing more. The next thing she knew, she was waking up in a set from Northern Exposure.

She tried to pull herself up to a sitting position, but it was too much for her. She fell back onto the pillow. Naomi snorted and rolled onto her side. Julia lay still until the woman's breathing became regular again.

Once more, she worked her way to a sitting position, and this time managed to get her arms in place to prop herself up. She was still in the same Levi's and sweater she had been wearing all week.

She spent a moment gathering what little strength she had, then silently swung her stockinged feet out from under the covers and onto the wood floor. Her head pounding unmercifully, Julia glanced back to check that Naomi was still asleep, then shakily got to a standing position. Nausea came over her in waves, and she had to struggle to keep her feet. Fighting off a strong urge to vomit, she slowly moved to the window to look outside.

The glass was old and wavy, but through the trees she could see a postcard view of a large, deep blue lake. Brilliant sunlight played off the ripples, hurting her eyes, but the scene was so beautiful that she couldn't look away.

She tried to figure out where she was. Obviously this one some sort of fishing lodge or cabin somewhere in the North, but apart from that, she didn't have a clue.

The window was sealed shut by weathering and layers of shellac, but there was a tiny space between the glass pane and the frame where the old wood had dried and contracted. Putting her face to the sliver of opening, Julia felt a cool draft, laden with the tangy scent of pine. Taking deep breaths of the sweet, free air made her feel a bit steadier and her nausea eased by degrees.

A movement caught her eye as two men came into view from the front of the building, heading toward the lake. She caught her breath: even from this distance, there was no mistaking the profile of Brady Keyes. He was talking to a tall, black man. They paused, staring off into the sky to their right. Brady's arms were crossed. He appeared serenely confident as he spoke. The other man listened and nodded, cradling a rifle in the crook of his right arm.

A third man emerged from the woods to their left and joined them. Brady listened to him for a moment, then said something while gesturing and pointing to various locations beyond Julia's view. The third man nodded and went back into the woods, while Brady and the other man continued their conversation.

With the nausea under control, Julia made her way around the edge of the room, past an antique dresser with a fun house mirror on top, beneath the coconut masks who still seemed to be watching her every move. Stopping at the six-panel door, she listened intently for several minutes, but heard nothing. Carefully, she tried the knob. The door was locked.

"Where'd you think you'd go, even if it was open?" Naomi's voice was raspy.

Julia laid her head against the door. "The hell away from here."

"Look, girl...you don't know where you are, you don't know what you're dealing with, and you look like shit to boot. Why don't you just lay back down and sleep it off?"

"Why don't you tell me where I am and what I'm dealing with?" Julia turned to face Naomi, who was propped up on one elbow. "And how the hell did I get here, anyway?"

Naomi rubbed her face with her free hand. "Well, I'd like to tell you where you are, but I'm not exactly sure myself. It was dark when we got here. All I know is that we're somewhere in Canada."

"Canada?" Julia wobbled back to the bed and sat down.

"Yeah, I can see you've heard of the place. Hockey teams and maple trees, and lots of snow."

"What am I doing in Canada?"

"Can't say exactly. But I did hear Roy say that if all goes well, you'll be back with your old man soon."

Julia blinked disbelievingly. "Are they holding George, too?"

"Don't think so. I heard he's bringing something to the guys."

Julia began to piece things together. She was glad to hear that George was going to be here, but she was worried about why. He must be delivering some sort of contraband for Brady, drugs or cash or something of that kind. Whatever it was, it was certainly illegal. What would happen to them then? She didn't think these men would just let them go, and even if they did, what if George had gotten himself involved in some serious crime?

"How did I get here, Naomi?"

"I guess you wouldn't remember. You was out like a light the whole way."

"You drugged me?"

"It wasn't me. One of Roy's men bought the food. I just fetched it in to you."

"So you didn't know it was drugged?"

Naomi shrugged. "I figured it was something like that. They just told me that you'd be taking a little nap and to get my things together for a trip."

"Why didn't you tell me?"

"Would you have eaten it if you knew there was something in it?"

Julia feigned hurt. "I thought we were friends."

"You may be a nice lady and all, but I don't work for you. I take my orders from Roy, and don't you get any ideas to the contrary."

Julia kept playing the injured party. Naomi sighed and sat up. "Look, let me see if I can scrounge up some coffee in this joint. You need to go to the can?"

Julia nodded. Naomi got up and pulled her coat from the hook next to the door. She knocked twice and an accented voice came through the door. "Waddaya want?"

"It's Naomi. Open the door. The lady needs to pee."

The door handle rattled for a few seconds. Finally the door squeaked open and a Latino appearing face poked in. "Make it fast," the man said in a thick Spanish accent.

"I'll make it any way I want, asshole," Naomi said. "Where's Roy?"

The man glared. "He's in the kitchen."

Sitting down with a coffee and staring out the window, Julia was beginning to feel halfway human again. She'd managed to wash up in the tiny bathroom while Naomi was in the kitchen. Now, sipping the hot brew and with the cool air from the window blowing gently on her face, Julia decided she might live after all. Naomi was slouched on her bed, playing solitaire and complaining about the lack of TV.

A commotion started outside. Several men scurried past the window, making for the back of the cabin.. A few seconds later, Julia heard an airplane. At first she became excited, thinking maybe George was arriving, but as she listened, her heart sank.

It was obviously a single engine plane.

Chapter 10

George leveled the aircraft at 20,000 feet and trimmed for the optimum cruise speed of 240 knots. Ordinarily he would have set the autopilot to assist with the 2½ hour flight, but he couldn't relax anyway, so he maintained manual control. It had become quiet aft. Haley was already snoozing and the Judge was glued to the window, admiring the rich brown and green patchwork of farmland that made up most of Michigan's thumb.

George hoped Haley would remain asleep for the duration of the flight. He was liable to get restless if he woke up, and to wander up to the cockpit. Then he'd sit in the right seat and ask to take the controls for a while. George didn't feel like giving a flight lesson today. In fact, he hoped he could avoid having to face Haley again altogether.

He reached around behind his seat and pulled the little curtain shut, isolating the cockpit from the passenger compartment. The curtain wasn't standard equipment in the King Air C90A, but Haley had installed it to maintain privacy when required. George slid the flight bag out from behind the copilot seat and placed it on the floor between the two seats. He reached down to unzip it and fished around inside for the remote control that would activate the smoke device. He pulled it out and pushed the bag back into place behind the seat.

There was a sliding on/off switch on the side of the remote, and a button on the front, just below a red LED display that would light up when the control was active. George turned it over in his hand, musing idly. One push of the button would alter his life forever... When he next checked the altimeter, *Haley's Comet* had lost 150 feet of altitude. George slipped the control into his shirt pocket and returned his attention to flying.

They were crossing the Straits of Mackinaw when Haley slid open the curtain and stuck his head in the cockpit. "Just wanted to see if you were awake up here, George."

George forced a laugh. "It's not that long a flight. Besides, it's just too nice out to miss any scenery." He hoped Haley would be satisfied and return to his guest. Instead he moved farther into the cockpit, bracing his hands on the backs of the two seats.

"You're absolutely right. Damn, that is a great view of the bridge."

"Yes, sir. Never get tired of that sight." Even under these circumstances, George had to admit that the Straits provided a spectacular view on a clear spring day.

"I hope the weather stays like this all weekend."

"You'll have fun even if it turns on you. You can show the Judge around your favorite watering holes in Fort Hope."

Haley chuckled regretfully. "My liver will only stand a couple of beers these days." He turned around and glanced back at Strand. "Speaking of beer, I'd better see if Albert is accommodated." George hoped that Haley would pull the curtain shut again as he withdrew, but he didn't.

George began reducing power for the descent into Sault Saint Marie, Canada, a necessary stop to receive Canadian customs clearance. As they dropped below 10,000 feet, the mixed pine and hardwood forests began to take on some definition. At 5,000 feet, he watched the cars crawling up I75, just south of the border. The traffic was probably due to vacationers getting an early jump on the weekend. He wished he was one of them.

Twenty minutes later, they were sitting on the airport ramp, waiting for the Canadian Customs Agents to inspect the airplane. This routine always made George nervous, but it was especially intense today, given the smoke device stuck inside the left engine nacelle. He hoped that once they found out who the passenger was, their inspection would be cursory.

Within 30 minutes, they had finished with customs, topped off the fuel tanks, filed their Canadian flight plan, and were ready to go. As soon as Haley and the Judge returned from using the facilities in the terminal, George fired up the two 550 horse power Pratt & Whitney turbines, and requested clearance to taxi to the active runway. Five minutes later they were airborne again, and George's stomach was in knots.

They were at 10,000 feet when Lake Ogaki came into view on the horizon. George picked it out from among the dozens of other lakes dotting the landscape by its size and unusual shape: from the air it almost looked like a sitting rabbit. He had studied Brady's charts and aerial photographs carefully, and he felt certain he knew every square mile of the immediate area.

He wasn't looking forward to making a single engine landing at the grass strip built years ago behind the camp where Brady was holed up. Although it was technically long enough to accommodate *Haley's Comet*, George's main concern was the surrounding dense pine forest, with trees topping 100 feet. A missed approach could spell disaster.

George pulled the remote control device from his pocket. He slid the switch to the on position, and the LED lit up. He glanced back at Haley and Strand: they were talking and laughing, already in the mood for their weekend. George forced himself to think of Julia. If he didn't do this thing, he might never see her again. He pushed the button, half-hoping it wouldn't work.

A wisp of smoke began trailing behind the left nacelle. A few more seconds and it was throwing off billowing, black clouds. Before George could say anything, Haley shouted, "George! What's going on?"

"I'm afraid we have a problem, sir." George kept his voice as calm and professional as he could. "It appears we have a fire in our left engine."

"So, what the hell are we going to do now?"

"First, sir, I need you to both to buckle in. Then I'm going to shut down the engine and feather the prop. If that doesn't put it out, we've got to find some place to put down, quick."

Haley looked out the window at the dense forests below, broken only by the myriad of lakes and rivers. "You didn't happen to install pontoons on this thing back in Sault Saint Marie, did you George?" He tried to force a laugh, but only managed a hacking rasp. So far, Strand had said nothing. George checked over his shoulder, and saw that the Judge was white as a ghost.

George had secured the engine, but clouds of black smoke kept streaming out. "It's not going out, Mr. Haley. I'm going to have to find some place to land before the fire reaches the fuel tank."

"Where, George? Where?"

George still hadn't spotted the grass strip. "I'm going to descend toward that lake. Maybe there is a road or something we can land on."

"It doesn't look like it. Can we land on the water?"

"Only as a last resort. At the very least, we'd lose the aircraft."

Haley reached over to put his hand on the Judge's shoulder. "It'll be all right, Albert. George is an excellent pilot. He'll put it down someplace and help will be here in no time." Haley turned to George. "Have you radioed our problem and our position to ATC?"

"Yes, sir," George lied. He'd flipped off the communications radio and was repeating a mayday call into a dead mike. He had also not activated his flight plan, so there would be no traffic controller following the flight. "I've done all I can. I'm going to prepare for an emergency landing. Have you both got your seatbelts on?"

Strand already did. Haley double checked it for him, and then buckled himself in. He looked out the window at the approaching tree tops. "Have you spotted anything yet, George?"

"Not yet." They were at three thousand feet and George still hadn't seen the strip. Brady had picked a desolate spot; there was nothing but thick forest everywhere. As they approached the lake, George strained his eyes along the southern edge, hoping to find some sign of the lodge.

Suddenly he saw a break in the trees. He figured that must be it, and headed toward it. Flashing over at two thousand feet, he saw the strip, in a valley between two small hills, or rather swells in the landscape. Just past the north swell, about half a mile, he spotted the lodge. He could just pick out shapes of people running toward the airstrip. He hoped Haley wouldn't notice them.

He yelled back in the passenger compartment, "We just passed over what looks like a private airstrip. I don't see it on the charts, but I'm sure that's what it is. Whatever it is, it's our best shot, so I'm going to set up for a landing."

Haley yelled back, "Are you sure we can get there?"

"It'll be tight." The runway ran from the southeast to the northwest. George had passed over it from the south to the north and entered into a right bank to set up for a right-hand base leg into it. The ripples on the lake indicated a fairly stiff breeze coming straight out of the northwest, allowing for a very slight crosswind.

He kept his turns shallow. The big twin was sluggish operating with a single engine and a feathered propeller, so he had to be careful not to lose airspeed too quickly. A stall at this stage would be fatal. He turned on final, lined up with the strip, and dropped the landing gear. He would be coming in over the tall pines to a relatively short runway, so he increased his descent rate. When he was sure he had the runway made, he applied full flaps and cut back power a little. He could see a vehicle racing along the side of the runway, probably to be at the end to greet *Haley's Comet* after her rollout.

Passing over the last of the pines, George chopped the power and the plane sank rapidly toward the runway threshold. Even with the light crosswind, landing on one engine was tricky and he had his hands full keeping lined up with the runway. Trying to keep the nose high and flare for a gentle, soft field touchdown ate up a lot of runway. Before he knew it, almost a third of the strip was behind them, so he pulled back on the wheel until the stall horn sounded and dropped the last three or four feet onto the grass. The hard landing caused the plane to swerve as it dug into the soft ground, but George danced on the rudder peddles and managed to keep from going off the runway.

A military-style jeep sat at the far end, which was approaching rapidly. Men jumped out and scattered to either side, not sure if the plane would stop in time. George glanced out the side window and noticed the trees speeding by. He'd increased pressure on the brakes carefully but firmly, trying to bring the aircraft to a stop without skidding, but now he pressed down harder and reduced the flap angle to put more weight on the wheels.

The airplane finally came to a stop, the nose dropping down and then bouncing back up, not five feet from the jeep. When the plane stopped moving, George looked out at the jeep and saw Brady Keyes, sitting alone and staring back, the trace of a smile creeping across his face. They studied each other for a few seconds, then George turned around to check on how his passengers were doing. Strand and Haley were both pale, but they seemed to be all right. With trembling hands, George shut down the airplane and undid his seatbelt and shoulder harness.

Chapter 11

Smoke was still billowing out of the left engine and drifting past the windows when George entered the passenger compartment, Haley was kneeling beside Strand, helping the older man to unbuckle his seatbelt.

"Are you okay, Judge?" George asked.

"He's all right," Haley replied, "just a little shook up."

George thought that Strand looked more than shook up. The judge was staring blankly at Haley, making no effort to help with the buckle. His arms hung loosely at his sides, and a trail of spittle dripped from his chin. George wondered if he might have had a stroke.

As soon as he'd got the seatbelt loose, Haley grabbed Strand's shoulders and spoke directly into his face. "We're safe, Albert, but we've got to get out of the plane." He turned to George. "Help me get him on his feet."

George obediently grabbed Strand's left arm and hefted him up. The movement seemed to bring him to his senses. He looked at George, "Nice job, young man."

George breathed a sigh of relief, but knowing what was waiting for them outside of the plane, he couldn't answer. He just nodded back.

As far as Haley was concerned, this was still an emergency landing. "Come on, George, we've got to get Albert out of here."

Before George could answer, Strand said, "Jack, who are those men out there?"

Several men were standing by the door. Some of them were armed. Haley stared at them. "George, did we land somewhere we weren't suppose to? Is this some sort of military base?"

George looked at the floor. "Like you said, we'd better get out quickly, sir."

Jack Haley's business career had spanned thirty successful years. He was nobody's fool. "What's going on, George? There's something you haven't told me, isn't there?"

Someone banged on the fuselage. Outside, men were shouting for the door to be opened. Haley glared at George. "You were expecting this."

"Sir, I think we'd better do as they say." George released Strand and moved to the door.

Haley wouldn't let it drop. "You owe me an explanation. Tell me what's happening."

George didn't reply. What could he have said? He unlatched the door, lowering it to the ground. Brady's face came into view. "Welcome to Lake Ogaki, Little Wing. Why don't you introduce your guests."

Haley said angrily, "You know this man? You'd better tell me what's happening, now!"

George looked back at Haley and Strand. "I'm sorry, sir. I had no choice." Then he stepped off the plane and said to Brady, "Where's my wife?"

"First things first." Brady pushed George aside. "Juan, Tony. Escort our guests off the airplane."

George started to protest, but Roy Lassiter grabbed his arm. "Take it easy, motherfucker."

Juan stepped into the plane, pointing a 9mm at Haley and Strand. Tony stood just outside the door and said in heavily accented English, "*Por favor, Señors,* get out of the airplane."

Strand looked at Haley. "Jack, what do these people want?"

"I don't know," Haley said, before turning to Tony. "Who are you people? Why should we do anything you say?"

"Because we have guns, Señor, and you do not. Now, get off the fucking plane before Juan becomes upset and shoots you."

Haley studied the gun Juan was holding, then glared at Tony. "All right, all right. We're coming."

Haley helped Strand past Juan and down the steps to where Brady waited. "Well, Judge, you don't look so authoritative right now."

Strand straightened himself and ran his fingers through his thinning white hair. "To whom am I speaking?"

"You wouldn't know me if I told you," Brady said. "But you might have heard of my employer."

"And who might that be?"

"Carlos Santez."

Strand looked puzzled. "I don't—"

"He is a relative of Hector Santez. Does that name ring a bell, Judge?"

Haley turned pale. Things had looked bad, and now they looked worse. "You remember, Albert, that scumbag drug dealer you put away a couple of years ago?" His voice held no hint of bravado, now.

Judge Strand drew himself up. "You people are associated with the Santez drug operation?"

"That's right, Judge. And now you and your friend here are going to be a part of it too. Won't that be fun?"

"What do you want with us?"

"Nothing, really. You'll be enjoying our hospitality until our respective employers complete a little transaction."

"You're holding us for ransom?" Haley glared at George, who was looking for a hole in the earth to swallow him up. "What is your share, George?"

George started to stammer an answer, but Brady interrupted. "George is no longer your concern, Mr. Haley. You need only to be concerned with me, and the answer to your question is no, we are not holding you for ransom. You and your esteemed friend here are prisoners of war."

"War? What the hell are you talking about?"

"The war on drugs." Brady and Roy both laughed, loudly.

"I figured as much," Haley said. "So, now what happens? You're going to kill us because we fight that war to protect the minds of our citizens?"

"You fight that war *because* of the minds of your citizens. And you are losing it for the same reason. We simply supply a product they demand."

"How long do you plan on holding us?" Haley said.

"Until our employers complete their transaction."

Then Brady said to Tony, "You and Juan, escort these two to the jeep and detain them." He turned to Roy. "You, George and I will follow in the other car."

Tony pushed his gun into Haley's back. "Into the jeep, Señor."

As they skirted around the wing toward the Jeep, Haley kept his eyes on George. George wished there was some way he could explain, but it was useless. Whatever he said, Haley would never believe him. He stared at the smoke that was still wisping gently from the engine nacelle.

Tony herded Haley into the back seat and climbed in alongside. He motioned for Strand to get into the front, next to Juan. Juan started the jeep, wheeled around and headed back down the trail. The other men took off after them on foot.

Brady grabbed George's arm and pulled him toward the car. As they walked, he smiled and said, "Well done, man! You see, we have learned something in these past twenty years."

George stopped in his tracks. "If you've harmed Julia in any way—"

"You know something? You wouldn't do a damn thing no matter what I did, so cut the macho bullshit. Just be grateful that your wife is okay and that you'll both be under the protection of Santez. I'm looking forward to being together again, *compadre.*"

"Well, I'm not. You have fucked up my life beyond belief. I've betrayed a man I respected, become an international kidnapper, and now I have to tell my wife that we're going on the lam for the rest of our lives. I'll be amazed if she doesn't tell me to pound sand up my ass."

"If she told you that," Brady said softly, "it would be a great disappointment to me. You two were the last hope I had for true love."

Naomi scrambled up from her bed, scattering playing cards on the floor. "What's going on?"

"I don't know." Julia was at the window, straining to identify the airplane that had just passed over, but it was obscured by the trees.

"I'm going outside. You stay put." Naomi banged on the door and yelled for Ricardo to open it.

Julia paid no attention. She'd managed to catch a glimpse of the plane as it turned to the right over the lake, and now her heart was thumping wildly. It was *Haley's Comet* after all, but only one propeller was turning; the other was feathered and smoke was streaming from the engine. If George was flying it, he was in trouble.

The plane banked to the right again and disappeared over the tall pines at the east end of the lake. She returned her attention to the room. Naomi was gone. Julia went to the door and stood by it for a few seconds. She heard nothing, so she tried the doorknob. It turned. She eased it open and poked her head outside. The guard's chair was empty. No sounds came from anywhere in the house.

Julia crept through the living room. It was a typical-looking male retreat, constructed from knotty pine and strewn with a hodge podge of old patio furniture and neon beer signs. A handful of poorly-painted wildlife scenes adorned the walls, while a moose head glared balefully at her from its mount over the well-used fireplace. She crept across the room, cursing under her breath when her foot pressed a creaky floorboard. She stepped over the board and made her way to the front porch, which was blocked by nothing more than a screen door swinging by its hinges, tapping against the frame in the gentle breeze.

Pushing the screen door open several inches, Julia peered

out. No one was in sight. She strained fruitlessly to hear the airplane engine, and then paced out onto the silent porch, alert to any danger.

A movement caught her attention. The man who had been sitting by her door came briskly around the side of an outbuilding, to the left of the main cabin. She shrank back against the screen door, ready to beat a hasty retreat back to the bedroom, but the man didn't come toward the house. Instead, he turned and disappeared around the side of the cabin.

Julia inched along the porch until she could see around the corner. The man was standing about fifty yards behind the cabin, looking down an old two-track road. He appeared to be waiting for something. She watched him for a while, withdrawing quickly two or three times when he turned to glance toward the house.

She took stock of the situation. The main cabin faced north, looking out on the lake she'd noticed when she first woke up here, beautiful and glittering in the early spring sun. The outbuilding to the west appeared to be a smaller version of the main cabin, about thirty feet square. Perhaps it was a guest house. To the north of the outbuilding was a three-sided wood shed. Firewood was piled high on one side, while an old outboard motor, shovels and rakes, several coils of rope, gasoline containers and oil cans occupied the other. The sparse lawn ran down to where the water lapped against the transom of an upside-down rowboat pulled three-quarters of the way out of the water. The entire compound appeared to occupy a huge horseshoe-shaped clearing in the big pine trees, although several of the largest trees stood here and there on the property.

A familiar voice drew her attention to the rear of the cabin again. Naomi appeared, walking on the two-track toward the man who had been standing there.

"They be coming, Ricardo. Better get back and check on the woman."

"She's all right. I want to see the faces of the Judge and the other one."

"You'll have plenty of time to see 'em. Go and check on her, damn it."

The sound of an engine announced an approaching vehicle. That seemed to melt Ricardo's resolve, and he turned and trotted toward the house. Julia's heart pounded as she retreated back into the cabin, taking care not to slam the screen door.

She banged her foot on the leg of the ancient sofa, and—swearing to herself— hobbled into the bedroom. She was just closing the door when Ricardo opened the screen door to the living room. She prayed he wouldn't notice the movement. She limped to the chair in front of the window and sat down, trying to control her breathing.

The bedroom door crashed open. Ricardo stood at the threshold, looking at the handle and muttering to himself in Spanish. Julia's heart skipped a beat. He knew that the door had been left unlocked. His eyes flicked toward Julia, who tried to pretend nothing had happened.

"Yes? What do you want?"

Before he could answer, Naomi appeared behind him. "Get out of the way, bean boy."

He turned and said something in Spanish.

"Honey, I don't understand a word you're saying."

Ricardo shook his head, then repeated in English, "You left the fucking door unlocked."

"Hey, you were the last one outta here."

"You left the fucking door unlocked. I should tell your Roy."

"Tell him anything you want, greaseball. Who's he gonna believe? I'll tell him you were coming on to me and he'll kick your ass. Now get out of my way." Naomi pushed past Ricardo, who slammed the door and locked it.

Naomi continued to curse Ricardo, but Julia ignored her. She was peering at the jeep that had just pulled up in front of the guest house, and straining to make out who was in it.

Chapter 12

"Honey, you're gonna bust something, thinking that hard."

Julia was barely aware of Naomi's words. She was still reeling from the shock of seeing two men escorted into the guest house at gunpoint. One of the men was Jack Haley, a close friend of her fathers. The other man looked vaguely familiar, but she couldn't place him. Of the two, Haley seemed to be holding up better to the ordeal. His companion looked frail and shaken.

She searched for George, but couldn't see him. Who had been flying the plane? Surely it had to be George, but why wasn't he with Haley and Strand?

"Hey, girl! Are you with me?"

Julia looked up at Naomi standing over her. "Yeah. What?"

"I think you're gonna be getting out of here."

"What do you mean?"

"Last night, Roy told me a plane was coming today, and that I should have you ready to go."

"Go where?"

Naomi shrugged. "How the hell do I know. Just get all your shit together."

"I was snatched out off the street, remember? Nobody bothered to forward my luggage."

"Don't be getting an attitude with me. I didn't have nothing to do with it. Just be ready to go, okay?"

Julia glanced around the room. "I don't see why I should. I'm getting kind of fond of this place...unless you wanted to tell me what's going on, of course."

Outside, a car door slammed. Through the window, she saw George, Brady Keyes, and the man Brady had been talking to earlier. Her husband looked miserable as he accompanied the other two men up the porch steps.

Julia couldn't help it: she let out a scream: "George!"

Approaching at the main house, George saw that the first jeep was parked behind the building. The vehicle was empty. He turned to Brady and demanded, "Where are Haley and the Judge?"

"You just gotta know everything, don't you?" Brady sneered.

"I want to be sure they're all right."

"I told you they were."

"I'd prefer to see for myself," George said.

"Well, you're going to have to trust me."

The car pulled up to the side of the cabin, and all three got out. As they stepped onto the porch, he heard his wife's voice calling his name.

"Julia!" he shouted in answer. "Where are you?"

Lassiter snorted. "Isn't that sweet. The love birds are calling each other."

George was already through the screen door and scanning the living room. "Julia, where are you?"

Brady followed him in. "Take it easy. We'll get her." He nodded to Ricardo.

Ricardo opened the door and Julia burst through it, ran to George and threw her arms around him. He couldn't remember when she'd squeezed him so tight.

George hugged her, burying his face in her hair. Holding

her in his arms again, his heart sang and ached at the same time.

They pulled apart and gazed at each other. Brady and the others looked on. Brady was smirking. "Do you mind?" George said to them. "We'd like to be alone for a few minutes."

"Later. Right now, we've got some business to attend to." Brady turned to Naomi, who was standing near the bedroom doorway. "Why don't you help Mrs. Ashton get ready while I have a quiet chat with her husband."

George took a step closer to Julia. "She stays with me."

"This is all very touching, but like I said, you and I have some business to attend to." Brady had put on his serious face. "Naomi," he yelled.

Naomi came over and tentatively put her hand on Julia's shoulder. "Come on, honey. Let the boys have their private time."

Julia shrugged off Naomi's hand and glared at Brady "Go ahead, George. I'll be all right." She turned and went back into the bedroom with Naomi.

"I'll be back soon," George said. Turning to Brady, he snapped, "What now, Keyes?"

"Roy, stay here with Ricardo." Brady motioned for George to follow him.

The kitchen was sparsely furnished: an old refrigerator, a clean but well used electric cooktop and oven, knotty pine cabinets and a faded red linoleum floor. The table in the center was covered with a worn checkered tablecloth. Sitting on the cloth was a brown leather briefcase. Brady indicated for George to take a seat. George was tempted to refuse, just to be obstinate, but he was tired from the flight. He pulled out one of the plastic covered chairs and sat down.

"Can I buy you a beer? I'd say you've earned one." Brady opened the refrigerator.

"I assume I'll be flying again in a while, but you go ahead. You're probably used to drinking alone, right?"

Brady ignored the jibe. "How about a cup of coffee?"

"Skip the bullshit. Let's just do what we have to do, and then Julia and I will be on our way."

Brady looked hurt. "You could be a little friendlier, especially since we're going to be business partners."

"I told you to cut the bullshit. I'm just as much a hostage as Haley and Strand."

"I think you'll be pleasantly surprised when you get to Colombia. Any friend of mine is a friend of Carlos. And you've done a big favor for him. You won't find him ungrateful."

"Friends don't kidnap friends. And what I did wasn't a favor."

"You did what you did. Now you're about to begin a new phase of your life. You'll get used to it."

Brady opened the briefcase and pulled out a manila folder and series of aeronautical charts. He flipped open the folder and pulled out a sheet of paper. "This is the flight plan to Colombia, including the fuel stops."

George studied the paper as Brady explained. "You'll clear customs at Chippawa County Airport, then on to Detroit to spend the night and pack up your things. On Saturday, you'll fly to Atlanta, then to Miami. You leave Miami and head out east until you're outside the twelve mile limit, then head south to Cuba. As you approach Havana, contact air traffic control and give them the information indicated here." Brady tapped his finger on a second piece of paper. "They'll be expecting you. After fueling, you'll head directly to Colombia, landing at Santa Marta first. Be sure to give air traffic control there the same information you gave to Havana. Finally, you'll fly to Medellin, where Santez's men will meet you and escort you to the compound. Got it?"

George nodded.

"You'll notice that all the headings, mileage and estimated time between waypoints, and radio frequencies are listed, along with the special identifying code to be used with air traffic controllers in Havana and Santa Marta." Brady paused and handed George the charts. "Here are all the maps for the airspace you'll be flying through. Any questions?"

"Yeah. Who prepared this?"

"You're not the only pilot Carlos has working for him."

"So why didn't this other guy do the job?"

"Somehow, I doubt that Haley and Strand would have wanted to get on his plane."

George thought of another objection. "What do I do when they arrest me in Sault Saint Marie for kidnapping a business man and a Federal judge?"

"You were never expected to stay the weekend with Haley and Strand, remember? Nobody will know that they're missing until we make our announcement on Sunday. By then, you'll be safely out of the country."

George still had trouble believing Brady would just let them go. "How do I know you won't make your announcement a little early? That would save Santez some money."

Brady studied George for a moment. "It may not be mutual, but I still think of you as a friend. You and I operate from different perspectives, that's all. You're still hooked on that sixties altruistic bullshit, but you're wrong. No one does anything without thinking of themselves first."

"And you'd be an authority on the subject of altruism," George said, "based on your personal experience."

"Touché." Brady grinned. "Still, I've carved out a very comfortable life in Colombia by doing jobs like this, by taking care of my obligations to Carlos. Now I'm taking care of you."

That didn't surprise George. Brady was a master manipulator. He'd take care of people who proved useful to him, but if push came to shove, he would always look out for himself first. It reminded George of the passionate debates they used to have, back in the old days. To Brady, man's animal instincts for survival were what mattered, while love was just an ideal to which the weak could cling for comfort in a harsh world. Sacrificing friends might not be his pastime of choice, but if he had to, he'd do it without regret.

"Anyway," he continued, "you know where we are. Believe

it or not, my plans don't involve an armed stand-off against the Mounties."

An intriguing idea, George thought. "A stand-off is what you'd get, if I turned myself in."

"And spend the rest of your life in prison?"

"That's a given. It's just a matter of deciding on the kind of prison."

Brady guffawed. "You really have no idea how we live, down in Colombia. Anyway, it wouldn't just be you, risking prison. You wouldn't want Julia to be involved, would you?"

"Of course not."

"Well, she is. You brought Haley and Strand to us, and no one knows that Julia was held against her will. You'd both be implicated."

George considered the matter and came to the only conclusion he could. "When can we leave?"

Brady scooped up the charts and packed them back into the briefcase. "There's no reason for you to be here. Grab your wife and get the hell out."

He slid the case across the table. George picked it up. "Gee, thanks Brady, you've done so much for me already, and I get to keep the briefcase too?"

"Poke fun if you like," Brady said. "You'll change your tune soon enough. That briefcase is only the beginning of all you're gonna get."

Chapter 13

George concentrated on the gauges as the two 550 horsepower engines revved up to 100% power. He was standing on both brakes, but *Haley's Comet* still slid forward under the tremendous thrust. He looked up toward the end of the field, which now seemed to have shrunk by about a thousand feet, then double checked the flaps, set for the minimum takeoff roll.

He glanced across at Julia, sitting in the right seat. Her eyes were fixed on the 100 foot pines just beyond the runway. She looked scared.

Keeping his voice light, George said, "It's okay, babe. I've gotten this thing out of tighter spots than this."

Julia smiled at him, but he could tell it was forced.

With the engines at full power and managing one last check of the gauges, he release the brakes and the straining airplane leapt forward. The first thousand feet flashed by, and *Haley's Comet* still showed no sign of wanting to leave the ground. He eyed the airspeed indicator anxiously as it crept toward rotation speed.

With about five hundred to go, he pulled the control wheel back and the nose rose skyward, but the main wheels were still bumping along the ground.

They reached the point where George no longer thought they could make it.

The airplane began to fly.

He retracted the landing gear and pulled the nose still further up, until the airspeed indicator showed that they were at the maximum angle of climb. With the nose so high, neither of them could see the trees, but George could've sworn that he felt some contact with branches as they rocketed skyward.

At two thousand feet, he released back pressure from the control wheel and watched the airspeed increase rapidly as the nose came down. When the Comet reached a more comfortable rate of climb, he relaxed slightly and looked over at Julia. "What'd I tell you? Piece of cake."

"Well, this cake is a little too fattening for me. I'll stick to yogurt from now on, if you don't mind."

George laughed, not so much at her joke, but more as a release now that he had her out of Brady's clutches. He reached over and grabbed her hand. "Honey, I'm so sorry this had to happen. I would have done anything to keep you out of it."

"It did happen and you couldn't have done anything about it, so don't worry about it." Then she looked away and added quietly, "Just don't let it happen again."

"Hey, I heard that." George feigned hurt.

"I meant for you to hear it," she lied. "But really, George, all that matters is that we're together again."

"You know I feel the same way—" He stopped himself and changed tack. "I'm afraid it's not over yet."

"What do you mean?"

He wasn't ready to discuss what happened next. "Listen, I've got to radio Toronto Center to let them know we're inbound to Chippawa County as an international flight. They'll arrange to have customs there when we land." He released her hand, trimmed the airplane for level flight, and tuned the communications radio to the proper frequency.

After raising the Center and informing them of his intentions, George slipped into silence. Julia didn't leave him in peace for long.

"George, what is going to happen now?"

He couldn't play the strong, silent type, not with Julia. She'd want to know everything, so he started at the beginning. He told her about the heist, and how Brady had gone to South America to live with his brother. He told her about Carlos and Hector Santez, and how Brady had blackmailed him into cooperating by kidnapping her. He explained the ruse to get Haley and Strand into Brady's hands before they could suspect anything was wrong. Then he told about the plans to fly to Colombia and the new life Brady had mapped out for them.

Finally, he told her why Brady believed that they would do what he expected them to. Through it all, Julia sat expressionless, staring out of the windshield.

When he had finished, she looked at him incredulously. "So we're criminals now? After all this shit, we're supposed skip the country and hide out for the rest of lives with one of the biggest drug lords in the world? Please tell me you're kidding."

He wasn't surprised by her response. That made what he was going to tell her next a little easier. "I'm not kidding about anything I've told you so far, but I haven't said that we were actually going to do anything that Brady expects."

She looked at him suspiciously. "Go on."

"I can't abandon Haley and Strand."

Her expression softened and she reached over and squeezed his arm. "Of course you can't. As soon as we get to the airport, we'll contact the authorities and let them know what's going on. They'll rescue Haley and Strand, everything will come out and we can get on with our lives." She paused. "That is, after we straighten out the little problem with your past."

George shot a look at her. "Little problem?"

"Come on, it's not that bad. It happened more than twenty years ago. The guard survived, and you weren't the one who shot him anyway, right?"

"Right, but—"

"So, Daddy will hire the best lawyer money can buy and he'll get you off with probation. Then we can start over."

"Julia, I appreciate what you're saying, but this is about more than my problem. If we involve the police, Haley and Strand are dead."

She sat quietly for a minute. "Okay, so what are you thinking?"

George was busy for a moment and couldn't answer: it was time to alert traffic at Chippawa County that he was on approach for landing. After making the announcement, he turned back to Julia. "We're going to be on the ground in a few minutes, so I don't have time to explain everything. But don't say anything to the authorities. Will you trust me on this?"

She looked at him. "I won't say anything. But you better have a damn good reason, George Ashton."

George didn't answer; he was too busy setting up for the landing.

They'd been sitting on the ramp for fifteen minutes by the time the Customs agent pulled up in his official car. He climbed out and sauntered toward the plane.

"If I'd known he was going to be this long, I'd have stretched my legs," Julia said.

"They don't like you leaving the plane before they arrive to inspect," George told her. "No telling what you might be doing, I guess."

As the uniformed man came closer, George saw that he was new—at least, George had never seen him before. He went aft to open the door. Julia followed and stood behind him. The Customs agent beckoned them down onto the ramp.

He launched straight into his business. "Where are you arriving from?" He spoke with a deep southern drawl that seemed completely out of place in this northern wilderness. George wondered how he'd ended up drawing this assignment. His name badge read Officer Wade.

"Fort Hope, Ontario," George lied.

"What is your citizenship?"

"We're both US citizens."

Officer Wade ignored George's claim for Julia's citizenship. "Ma'am?"

"United States," she said.

"How long were you in Canada?"

"Just a few hours," George said.

"What was your purpose?"

"I...we flew two passengers to a fishing camp on Lake Eabamet."

Wade paused for an extra second at George's stumble. "So this is a commercial aircraft?"

"Yes. The aircraft is owned by Haley Electronics. I'm employed by them."

"Do you have all the appropriate aircraft documents?"

"Yes."

"May I seem them?"

George was irritated by the request. None of the previous agents had ever asked for the aircraft documents. As he went back into the plane, he looked at Julia. He was nervous about leaving her alone with Wade, even for a few seconds.

As soon as George was gone, Wade turned his attention to Julia, "Are you the copilot?"

"No, I'm George's wife." Then she quickly added, "I often accompany him on flights like these."

"What did your husband say the flight was for?"

Julia knew that Wade must remember what George had said just a couple of minutes earlier. He was obviously checking to see if they both said the same thing.

"We took George's boss and his friend to Fort Hope. From there they ferry across Lake Eabamet to Mr. Haley's fishing lodge."

"When are you picking them up?"

This one threw her. She knew about the fishing camp, but she didn't know what the original arrangements for the trip had been. What if George contradicted what she said? Wade was waiting for the answer, so she'd have to be vague. "I believe George mentioned he was returning next week. I wasn't planning on going, so I didn't pay close attention."

Wade was looking at her carefully when George returned with a folder. "Here are the papers." He handed them to Wade.

As Wade thumbed through the documents, he asked George, "When are you retrieving your passengers?"

Julia caught his eye and gave a tiny shrug of her shoulders. George said, "Monday. Probably see you again then."

Wade's businesslike demeanor didn't so much as flicker. "Are you carrying any firearms, alcohol or drugs?"

"No. That is, nothing except the drinks tray. Airline-sized bottles Mr. Haley keeps onboard for his guests."

"Would you mind opening the cargo bay?"

George did as he was asked. Then he returned to Julia while Wade meticulously went through *Haley's Comet* . When he completed the inspection and was stepping out of the passenger compartment, he noticed the black mark that streaked across the engine nacelle, left by the smoke device. "Problem with your plane?"

George stared at the black streak for a second before answering. "Ah, no. Just burning a little oil."

"Looks like more than a little to me. You sure that engine is okay?"

"Yeah. But I'll have the mechanic look at it when we get back."

"It's your call, but I'm not sure I'd want to fly this thing like that."

"It's not a problem, Officer Wade."

"Whatever. It's your funeral." He paused for a minute to study George and Julia one last time with his hooded eyes. "Well, I guess I'm done here. You can leave whenever you're ready."

George thanked him and watched as Wade strode back toward his car. The fuel attendant arrived, and George told him to top off the tanks with Jet A. Then he guided Julia toward the lounge area of the fixed-base operation, so she could use the facilities while he got a weather update.

On their way to the building, Julia asked, "Do you think the Customs agent suspected anything?"

"I don't think so. If he had, he would have found some reason to keep us here. But he sure took his time inspecting the airplane."

Julia thought for a moment. "Maybe he sensed something wasn't quite right, but couldn't find a good enough excuse to detain us."

"Could be," George admitted.

"Are you going to tell me what's going on, now?"

"Not yet. Let's finish up and get airborne ASAP. I want to get the hell out of here."

Chapter 14

Setting a course of 210 and trimming for level flight at 10,000 feet, George stayed well below the altitude that would require him to file a flight plan. After surveying all the instruments, he engaged the autopilot and turned to Julia. She was looking at the heading indicator with a puzzled expression.

"You noticed that we're not on course for Detroit?" he inquired.

"I'm no navigator, but I'd swear we're headed more toward Chicago than Detroit. That wasn't part of Brady's plan, was it?"

"Nope. It's part of George's plan."

"Okay. I can already tell I'm not going to like this, but let's have it."

George spent a few seconds considering how to launch into what he had to say. "Brady was right about one thing: there was no way I'd have compromised Haley and the Judge unless I was properly motivated, and blackmailing me about my past wasn't enough. But as soon as Brady grabbed you, he had me over a barrel. I had to do what he wanted."

"Go on."

"Last week, I decided that I had to make things right. I don't care what happens to me, but the thought of betraying Haley makes me sick."

"You're going back for them, aren't you?"

"I've got to. Haley has been like a father to me. And both of them are among your father's closest friends."

"I don't care what my father or your father-figure thinks, you're not going to play some macho game and leave me a widow. We're going to turn this over to the authorities. They'll be able to handle it."

"Julia, there is no way that the police or anybody else could get those two out of there alive. No way. Brady will not go back to Santez empty handed. That's not something people in that world can afford to do."

"You're saying he's got nothing to lose?"

"Right. If the police assaulted that place, everybody would die."

"But they have special teams, don't they? They could mount some commando-style raid and get them out safely."

George snorted. "Remember Waco? Julia, this would be an international incident. There'd be so many cooks pissing in the soup that it wouldn't have a chance for success. Besides, Santez might have people on the inside. It happens, you know. Whoever we talked to, word could get back to the bad guys. Or if the press got hold of it, Brady would see the media coverage."

"What do you think he'd do?"

"Who knows? If Haley and Strand were lucky, he'd just move them somewhere else."

"It still doesn't have to be you."

"Yes, it does."

"Why? To atone for your past? That's a load of crap!"

Stung, George didn't answer immediately. It was true. He was looking for atonement, for forgiveness, for freedom. "Julia, you don't know what it's been like carrying this around with me for twenty years. A man almost died because of my stupidity."

"That would have happened whether you were there or not."

"I could have done something to stop it. It's too late, now. But it's not too late for me to do something to stop this."

They both fell silent, staring out of the windscreen, and

listening to the drone of the engines. George busied himself with flight tasks and after a few minutes had passed, he began again.

"There was something else about the heist."

"Yes?"

"Remember, I mentioned Steve, Rick, and Bobby? Last week, when I started hatching this plan, I knew I couldn't do it alone." He glanced over at her to check her reaction, but she was staring straight ahead, expressionless.

"I had no idea who to turn to until I thought of the guys. Trouble was, it's been twenty years. So I spent the better part of two days calling old friends and checking around, and by Tuesday, I'd tracked down Steve."

"Where?"

"Racine, Wisconsin. He's been living there for eight years."

"What's he do?"

"Sells insurance. Seems he's done pretty well for himself, financially."

"Is he married or anything?"

"Not married now, but he was."

"So you talked to him."

"I had a flight to Minneapolis Wednesday morning, and I managed a stop over in Racine. We had lunch."

"What was it like? I mean, seeing him after all these years?"

George smiled as he recalled the meeting. Brady had woven his spell over a relatively short period, but Steve had been George's friend since they were twelve. Seeing him again brought up all those memories: the good times, the scrapes they'd gotten into, even the hours they'd spent arguing about the impact the Social Coalition would have on society. "It was great. It was like we didn't miss a beat. I guess we both look a little different, but our heads were still in tune. We talked about everything. And I found out about Rick and Bobby."

"Where are they?"

"Rick lives in New York. He and Steve kept in touch all these years. He went to France after the heist. Lived on the left bank in Paris for a while, becoming an artist. He seems to have quite a reputation, and now he's back in the States."

"You seem pretty happy for him," Julia said.

"I loved that guy!" George smiled again. Rick had never been the most popular of their crowd and was certainly no athlete, but he was always eager to please and willing to try anything.

"What about Bobby?"

George's voice lowered. "Bobby died twelve years ago. He stayed with Steve when they were on the lam, living in Mexico for a while, then eventually Tucson. Something like what happened, it's there in your life forever. It eats you up. Steve and Ricky and me, we managed to move on. Bobby didn't."

"What happened?"

"He had a drug problem from way back when. After the heist, he started drinking too much as well. His health deteriorated until...well, you know, he just drank himself to death."

Julia reached over and squeezed George's hand.

He went on. "So, after Steve and I bullshitted about old times for a couple of hours, I told him about my problem And my idea."

"What did he say?"

"He gave it about two seconds of deep thought , then he said 'when do we go?' He couldn't wait to help out."

"Then he's even crazier than you," Julia said.

"You have to understand, we were like that." George showed her a pair of crossed fingers, shaking his hand for emphasis. "And like I said, something like that heist eats you up inside. I think Steve's looking for a reason to forgive himself. Anyway, he got in touch with Rick."

"And Rick jumped on board too?"

George considered for a moment. "I understand there was a certain amount of arm-twisting, but he agreed in the end."

"So, three middle-aged, out-of-shape hippies are going to take on an organized crime gang. What's your plan? A sit-down strike?"

"We're going in quietly. At night . We'll extract Haley and the Judge before anyone knows what is going on."

"Guns?"

"Steve owns a couple of handguns. And we'll have Kevlar vests."

"That makes me feel so much better," Julia said sarcastically.

George shrugged off the remark. "If we do this thing right, there won't be any shooting."

"That's what you thought about that art heist."

"Brady's not with us this time. If he hadn't lost his head, nothing would've happened. Besides, Steve and I have planned this out to a gnat's ass."

Julia fell silent for a few seconds. "Okay. Great. I'm in."

"No way. You'll stay hidden."

George could feel Julia's anger like prickles on his skin. Her voice when she spoke, however, was calm, almost emotionless. "I've been kidnapped, drugged and held hostage. I've been treated like unclaimed baggage. I've not only lost a week of my life, I've been cheated of a whole relationship with a man who is only ten percent available to me because he's ashamed of ninety percent of his life. I have just as much of a score to settle with Brady Keyes as you do. So make a choice. Either I'm in — or I walk away and come back with the Feds."

George nodded imperceptibly as he looked out at the Lake Michigan shoreline. South of Sleeping Bear Sand Dune, the land slipped slowly away under the port wing. Along the horizon to the west, he could just make out Wisconsin.

A deep calm crept through his bones. He was completely at one with the present moment, with the woman beside him and the plane around him — the two things he loved most in the world. All the moments of his life had brought him to this place and this time. No matter what happened for the rest of his days, this moment would live forever in his heart. For the first time in his life, George felt complete.

For this feeling, he would risk it all. "Okay. You're in."

Chapter 15

The fuel jockey guided *Haley's Comet* to a tie-down in front of the terminal at Meigs field, which was George's preferred airport in the Chicago area. It allowed him to avoid the congestion of O'Hare, and it was close to Lake Michigan: the north/south runway actually jutted out into the lake, making for a very scenic approach.

They deplaned and, after George gave instructions to the young man, hurried to the fixed-base operations. Although it was a clear, sunny seventy five degrees inland, the lake was still ice-cold and the brisk northeast breeze coming across the water was chilly. George greeted the woman behind the counter. "Hi, Lucy."

The silver-haired woman looked up from the paperwork she had spread over the counter. "George! How have you been? It must have been a couple of months, at least."

"It's been a while. Lucy, I don't think you've met my wife, Julia."

Lucy eyed Julia, making George a little uncomfortable at how ragged his wife looked. It didn't seem to be a problem for Lucy, though. "Pleasure to meet you, Mrs. Ashton. George's visits here are brief, but he's found time to tell us all about you."

"Please, call me Julia." She offered her hand across the counter.

Lucy accepted the handshake and smiled. "Of course, Julia."

George interrupted. "Lucy, I don't mean to be rude, but did you order that rental car for me?"

Lucy gave George an exasperated look. "Do I look like an idiot, George? Of course I did, right after you radioed. They should be here any time. They're usually pretty good."

"Thanks. It's just that we're in a bit of a hurry."

"So, what's new? You never have time to chat anymore."

"I'm sorry, Lucy."

"Are you back out right away?"

"No, we're going to stay for a couple of days." He caught her puzzled look, so he added, "Kind of a weekend perk from the boss."

The man from the car rental agency arrived. "Got a car here for Ashton?"

"That's us," answered George.

"Can you give me a lift back to the office? We're a little short-handed so no one could follow me over."

"Sure, but I have to make a phone call first. Can you wait a minute?"

"Yeah, I'll be in the car." The man glanced at the briefcase at George's feet. "That all you got?"

"That's it, but I'll take care of it, thanks." Then to Lucy. "There's still a phone in the pilot lounge?"

"As always, George."

He beckoned Julia into the lounge. "Steve's been standing by waiting to hear from me. He'll start down from Racine as soon as I let him know we're here."

✦

After they dropped the man off at the rental office, Julia exclaimed, "George, get me to a hotel and a hot bath immediately. I can't stand myself, so I can't imagine how you can."

"Well, I'm getting used to it."

Julia reached over and swatted him on the shoulder.

"But first, wouldn't you like to get a few toiletries and some clothes to change into?"

"You certainly know the way to a woman's heart. I guess I can stand myself for a little while longer."

They wound through the familiar streets of downtown Chicago, stopping at a couple of stores to get Julia the things she'd need for the next few days. Eventually they made their way to the Palmer House—more extravagant than they usually chose when they were paying their own way, but after everything Julia had been through, George felt she'd appreciate a little luxury.

They settled into the room and Julia headed for the tub. George stretched out on the bed and, in spite of the fact that his head was whirling with the events of the past week, he quickly fell asleep.

The telephone woke him. He sat up, trying to orient himself, and picked up the handset.

"Yes?"

"That you, Little Wing?"

George's stomach turned into a knot, until he recognized Steve Raimus's voice. It wasn't just Brady who had called him by that name. "Hey, Steve! Where are you?"

"In the lobby."

"Already? What time is it?"

"You call and I move, old buddy. It's about five-thirty. You sound like you were sleeping."

"Must have dozed off. Listen, can you give me a twenty minutes to wash up? How about if we meet you in the bar?"

"Sure. I'll go ahead and check in, and I'll see you then."

Steve hung up. George rubbed his face, stood up and went into the bathroom. Julia was checking herself in the mirror, adjusting her new dress.

He stood behind her and gave her reflection a long, admiring glance. "I was hoping I'd catch you before you put that dress on." He put his arms around her.

She turned in his embrace and kissed him. "There's no particular reason it has to stay on, is there?"

He hesitated, then mustered his willpower. "Steve just

called. He's waiting for us down in the bar. Let's go meet him, have some dinner, and get the hell back here. Waddaya say?"

"Alone?"

"Of course, alone. Unless you've got some kinky scene in mind, and you're planning on asking Steve to join in."

She pushed him away. George laughed. "I'll jump in the shower and be ready to go in ten minutes."

The hotel bar was filling up as Julia followed her husband inside. George scanned the room for a while, looking for Steve. "There he is." He indicated a tall, pleasant-looking man who was lounging in one of the paneled wall booths. "Raymass!"

The man in the booth looked across at them and stood up. "Little Wing!"

Steve Raimus had wavy, light brown hair and a thin face that was engulfed in a charming smile. Only his brown eyes looked sad. George grabbed his hand and pumped it vigorously.

"Steve, this is Julia."

Steve dropped George's hand and offered his to Julia. "What a pleasure to meet you."

His grip was firm. Julia found herself liking him already. "It's always fun to meet friends from George's youth."

Steve kept his eyes on her face. "Now I understand why George was so anxious to see you home safely. He was quite beside himself."

Julia found herself blushing at the compliment, and the reference to her kidnapping. "I think I was more worried about him, but I'm glad we're both here to meet with you."

George interrupted. "Hey, we can talk over dinner. I'm starved."

They left the bar and made their way to an Italian restaurant that Steve recommended. The place was several blocks away, so George had time to bring Steve up to date with all that had transpired since the two men had seen each other.

At the restaurant, George got down to business as soon as they'd ordered. "Have you heard from Rick yet?"

Steve glanced at Julia and raised an eyebrow. He looked distinctly uncomfortable. George explained: "Don't worry, Julia knows all about the little adventure we're planning. In fact, she's coming with us."

For a moment, Julia thought Steve would object, but his concerned expression melted into relief. "That's great! I'm sure we can use her help."

"When is Rick getting in?" George asked.

"Tomorrow afternoon. He wanted to join us tonight, but he had some things to take care of."

"It'll be great to see him. I miss the guy."

"What's he like?" Julia asked.

George turned to Steve. "Rick is very Zen, wouldn't you say?"

"Yeah. Zen with a fun-loving streak, and unbelievably mellow. Whatever came up, he'd adapt and take it in his stride." Steve grinned. "Maybe it came of being such a pot head."

George shrugged. "I've met people who got stoned way more than he did, and they were jerks. Anyway, I knew Rick from way back when. He didn't always smoke, but he was always a good friend to me."

Over the pasta, they discussed what they planned to do. Julia's concern grew as the details emerged. "So, let me get this straight: you're planning a dead stick landing into the same strip where we almost got killed trying to take off this afternoon?"

"We can't come in with power on, they'd be all over us before the plane rolled out."

"Well, even if they don't hear us, what if they see us? *Haley's Comet* isn't exactly a sparrow, you know."

"We'll come in low from the south at dusk. There'll be just enough light for me to see the field. At that time of day, everyone who doesn't enjoy being eaten by mosquitoes will be indoors."

"And if they're not?" she asked.

"The ridge between the field and the house will provide

cover. They won't be expecting any planes, so there's no reason for anyone to be around the field."

Steve echoed Julia's concern. "It doesn't sound like there will be much room for error."

George nodded. "If I miss the approach, we'll have to crash land." He speared a piece of tortelloni.

Julia remembered the dense forest. "We wouldn't stand a chance."

George chewed and swallowed. "You're talking worst case scenario. I've practiced power-off landings dozens of times. It won't be easy, but it's doable."

"Okay, but there's still a risk. Maybe Steve and Rick should get there some other way."

"There is no other way." George glanced at Steve. "There is only one two-track into that area and it is watched all the time. Even if we managed to get in undetected, we'd never get out. It has to be by air."

"It just seems—"

George interrupted. "Nobody has to come with me; I'd understand completely. But this is something I've got to do, and I'm going, come hell or high water."

"I'm in," Steve said.

When the waiter came by with the dessert tray, Julia ordered the cheese cake. "I don't know about you two, but I'm eating while I can."

George and Steve followed suit and when the desserts arrived, talk turned to the past, remembrances of the turbulent sixties, Viet Nam, and of course, Brady Keyes.

"You knew Keyes before I did. When did you meet him?" George asked Steve.

"I bumped into him at the Student Union one day. I recognized him from an art history class I was taking. He told me he was just auditing the class, which blew me away—I couldn't imagine anyone sitting through those tedious lectures if they didn't have to. We kind of hit it off, so we went out drinking a couple of times. As I recall, you joined us on one of those debacles, and the rest, as they say, is history."

They amused Julia for a while with anecdotes, but after

descriptions of the fourth or fifth or tenth drunken bout she'd had enough. "You two can stay here and relive your misspent youths if you want to, but I've had a long day. I'm going back to the hotel."

They both looked slightly embarrassed. "I'm tired too," George said. "We've got a lot to do tomorrow; we'd better all get some sleep."

That night, George seemed unusually hesitant in approaching her. For all the exhilaration of the rescue and the flight, there was a feeling of regret as well. Julia tried to reassure him, but she sensed that something had changed forever. The events and disclosures of the past few days had left them with a marriage that was more fractured than before, yet also more honest.

Their lovemaking was tentative and brief before both succumbed to exhaustion.

Chapter 16

They met for breakfast at the hotel restaurant. Saturday morning had started sunny, but now clouds were hurrying in, threatening rain. George brought his aeronautical charts so they could discuss the finer details of the rescue operation.

Steve gazed through the window, up at the sky. "What happens if the weather is poor tomorrow? Can we still fly?"

"Not if it's too bad. We'll be entering Canada illegally, which means flying on visual only. If it's solid overcast I'll never be able to find the airstrip."

"Why enter illegally?" Julia asked. "Can't we just reverse the process we went through yesterday?"

"They might search the plane again, and with what we're going to be carrying, we'd be finished before we got started. We can't take the risk."

"So how are we going to get in?" Steve asked.

George opened one of the charts and stabbed a finger at Lake Superior. "We're going to cross the lake at wave top level, pass over St. Ignace Island, and onto the mainland right between Nipigon and Rossport."

Steve peered at the chart. "Okay."

"I know the area," George continued. "There's nothing for miles in any direction. If we stay low we should avoid radar until we're deep enough inland that it won't matter. Unless we pass right over an RCMP patrol car, we should get in completely unnoticed."

"So, what if the weather doesn't clear in time?"

"I checked the Weather Channel, and called the local Flight Service Station for a weather briefing. This is just a typical spring cold front passing through. It should be out of here by the evening. A large Canadian high is right in back of it, and that's what's going to be dominating the weather for the next few days. It should be perfect."

They inventoried their supplies, including Steve's .38 caliber handgun and a tranquilizer gun that he said had belonged to his father, a former security guard. George made a list of extras and handed it to Steve. "Here's what we'll need. I need to stay here and work out the final details for the flight, so why don't you and Julia go shopping?"

"It'll be my pleasure, if Julia doesn't mind."

Julia looked doubtful for a moment but then she said, "Of course I don't, if you don't think I'll be in the way."

"Okay, that's settled." George put away his charts.

"Don't forget Rick's coming in to O'Hare later," Steve said.

"I'll pick him up and bring him back to our room, so meet us there when you're done. Then we can grab something to eat here in the hotel restaurant, and sack out early."

"That's a great idea." Julia pushed her plate away with a satisfied sigh. "Judging by breakfast, I'd say the people in the kitchen know what they're doing."

At two o'clock, George was sitting at the gate where Rick's plane was due. The flight from New York had been delayed forty-five minutes, having dodged the thunderstorms the front had produced over Michigan.

George gazed through the big glass walls at the delicate ballet of planes taxiing to and from the various runways, and marveled at the skill and dedication of the traffic controllers who moved the giant airplanes around one of the busiest airports in the world. If you weren't one of the pilots who flew in and out regularly—and in some cases, even if you were—O'Hare's myriad of runways and taxiways were mind boggling.

It was 3:15 p.m. by the time the big Boeing nosed up to the jetway and bobbed to a stop. Ground attendants swarmed the plane from all sides, performing their duties with varying degrees of intensity—some with vigorous energy, others with more deliberation, and still others with unconcerned detachment.

Eventually, passengers began emerging from the gate and entering the terminal. George watched carefully as each one appeared, idly speculating on their lives, until he saw a casually dressed man with thinning dark-blond hair, and enough remnants of Paul Newman-type good looks to make the soft fleshiness of the face and body seem incongruous.

Rick might be older and more mature, but George recognized him immediately. He yelled over the din of the crowd, "Rick, Rick, over here!"

Rick turned, spotted George, and gave a smile that involved his entire face. He broke out of the line and hurried over, ignoring George's offered hand to embrace him with both arms. "George! It's great to see you!"

George pulled back from the hug to look at Rick's blue eyes. "Rick, thanks for coming. I know it wasn't easy breaking away so quickly."

"You're right, it wasn't, man. But friendship is friendship, and it comes before business."

"Well, I can't tell you how good it is to see you. Having you and Steve along gives me the confidence I need to pull this off."

Rick's smile faded. "I only wish Bobby were here to round out the ol' gang."

"Yeah, I can't believe he's gone." George let his eyes drop. "We all miss him, but Steve more than anybody."

"Well, his passing wasn't in vain. It made me take a hard look at some of the habits I'd been developing. You won't believe me now, man. Clean as a whistle."

George looked up again. In spite of Rick's clear eyes and

winning smile, his overall appearance was not one of health and vitality. "That's terrific."

"Doing okay for an old fart, eh? Maybe looking a little thicker around the middle and thinner on the top, but not too bad."

"Not bad at all," George lied. "Come on, let's get out of here. We can catch up on the way to the hotel."

They merged with the flow of the crowd, heading for the baggage claim area. By the time they reached the parking lot, Rick was breathing like he'd just finished a marathon. As they got into the car, his face was flushed and he was sweating profusely, even in the relatively cool air. "Damn, it's been warm this spring, hasn't it?"

"Yeah," George answered unconvincingly. Even though he was happy to see Rick, he was beginning to think that it might not have been such a great idea to get him involved.

The ride back to the hotel was filled with talk about the old days, mutual friends and current events. Rick caught George up on his life. He had always had a predilection for art, he said, and while hiding out in Europe he'd spent some time studying in Paris.

He eventually returned to the US in the mid-eighties and managed to land a job with an advertising agency. By the end of the decade, he'd worked his way up to senior art director.

He'd never married, but had been living with a woman for the past eight years and had helped raise her two children, now in their teens. Aside from the obvious physical changes, Rick was still the same fun-loving, good-natured soul George remembered.

While Rick checked into the hotel, George went back to his room to see if Julia and Steve had returned. He found a note telling him that they'd gotten tired of waiting, and that he should join them down to the bar.

George had to wait for Rick before doing that, so he spent the time going through the bags of supplies Julia and Steve had purchased. They included four high-powered flashlights and a couple of penlights, spare batteries, camouflage clothing, a night scope, bolt cutters, several purse-sized mace applicators, rope, extra shells for Steve's gun, star flares, extra-strength insect repellent, and a couple of duffel bags to hold everything.

A few minutes later, Rick knocked at the door. "Holy shit! It looks like you're planning an invasion," he said as he entered, staring at the supplies spread out on the bed.

"Sort of brings back memories, doesn't it?"

"Yeah, but not good ones. I thought I was done with that crap."

"Well, this is for a good cause."

"That's what you said back then."

George smiled, "Come on, let's put this away."

Rick helped him put the things into the duffel bags. "So, where're the others? I'm looking forward to meeting Julia."

"They're down in the bar. I hope they haven't been there too long, if you know what I mean."

"Yep. I do. Let's go rescue them."

George and Rick wound through the sparse crowd to find Julia and Steve at the booth table that Steve had been at the day before. Steve was sipping a scotch; Julia, her usual tonic water.

Upon seeing Rick, Steve stood up and came out from behind the table to receive a hug similar to the one George had gotten at the airport. George realized how good it was to see the two of them together, and how lucky he was to have friends like these. Even after twenty-five years, they'd responded to his plea for help. It wasn't just a craving for adventure that lured them, although he suspected that they both still had a wild hair; he knew they were doing this out of their friendship for him. He felt gratitude and embarrassment in equal measure.

Rick turned to Julia and said, "Since you're the prettiest one here, I assume you're Julia."

She stood and offered her hand. "Hello, Rick. I'm pleased

to meet you. I've met more of George's old friends in the past week than...I don't know since when."

"Then you're finally getting to discover what a scoundrel he was."

"So far, it's no more than I already knew."

Laughing, they all sat down. George asked Julia, "How long have you been here?"

"About three hours."

"What...?"

"Well, maybe more like an hour, it just seems like three... we thought you guys would never get here."

George flicked a glance toward Steve, hoping he wouldn't take offence at the remark. "Rick's flight was delayed."

Rick chimed in, "So what else is new?"

George continued, "How'd the shopping go? It looks like you got everything on the list."

Steve answered, "Yeah, we got everything, but it was a pain in the ass. We had to go to two Army/Navy surplus stores, a hardware and a gun shop."

Julia added, "But we got to do a little sight-seeing along the way. Too bad it wasn't a nicer day."

"Well, it should be breaking up this evening," George said.

The waitress appeared. Steve ordered another scotch, while Rick asked for a beer. George settled on a tonic. He wanted to maintain a clear head until all this was over.

While they were waiting for their drinks, Rick piped up, "So, who called this meeting?"

Steve answered, "Little Wing, the vigilante."

Instead of smiling, George became defensive. "Nobody has to do this, you know."

"Lighten up, George," Steve said. "We all want to be here. You're not the only one with sins to atone for."

"I'm not trying to atone for any sins. I'm just trying to do the right thing. I need your help, but if you don't want to get involved, I'll understand. I'll do it myself if I have to."

Julia broke in. "George, your friends are here and that speaks for itself. But this may be tougher than you all realize. It's not too late to get the authorities involved."

Steve responded before George could. "I agree with George on that. The cops would turn it into a siege. If that happens, nobody there will make it out alive. The best we could hope for would be that Brady gets wind of what's coming down, and gets out of there first."

George, grateful for the support, said, "You see, Julia? I'm not crazy. Steve knows how Brady thinks. The only chance we have of seeing them alive is if we go get them ourselves."

Julia cast a hopeful glance in Rick's direction, who disappointed her by adding, "I'm afraid they're right. Brady can be a ruthless bastard. Carlos Santez sounds even worse. These drug lords have their tentacles everywhere; I don't doubt that Brady would be forewarned of a police rescue."

Julia sighed, "All right, I give up. But whatever we do, we have to do it as a team. No bickering or dissension, not like—"

She was interrupted by the arrival of the waitress with their drinks. George's mood shifted. "All right. Let's drink up and go get some food. I want to meet back in our room tonight early and go over the details."

"Since when did Little Wing become so task-oriented?" Rick asked.

George smiled. "Since I got back with you losers."

Chapter 17

George was out of bed and at his hotel room window, checking the weather as the steel-gray dawn crept over the city. The downtown buildings were rain-shrouded monoliths, looming over the early-morning traffic that splashed along the streets below.

The front that was supposed to have passed over by now was still firmly overhead. But there were twelve hours until departure, and he still felt confident that the clouds would clear out toward the north first. He turned away from the window and flicked on the Weather Channel, keeping the TV muted so as to not disturb Julia.

Their second night back together had been more intimate than their first, as they'd begun to share the events of the past week. George smiled at the sleeping woman as he remembered the quiet passion of the night before.

He could have lost her.

The thought of that made his heart ache, before it hardened with hatred for the man who'd put Julia in jeopardy, the man who was trying to destroy the life they shared.

Brady had always been the stronger man. George knew that. He also knew there'd been a time when he'd sought to ally himself with men stronger than himself.

Not any more.

Standing by the hotel room window, watching the silent

TV, he made a vow. Never again would he compromise the things he loved to appease the man he used to fear.

Windshield wipers shrieked against wet glass as they pulled into the parking area at Meigs Field. No one had commented on the weather, but Julia felt sure she wasn't the only one who felt concerned.

George pulled on the parking brake and killed the engine. "I'll go ask Lucy to have someone open the gate so we can pull onto the tarmac and load up the plane."

After he'd gone, everyone sat in silence. Finally, Rick said "George is worried about the weather, isn't he?"

Julia sighed. "He's still determined to go. And so am I."

"We're all determined," Rick said. "I just wondered if he'd mentioned the possibility of scrubbing the mission." He looked to Steve for support.

"Stop worrying," Steve said. "George knows what he's doing."

"Yeah, I know. The thing is, he's doing it, no matter what. That doesn't leave much wiggle room for a weather delay."

Julia kept her tone carefully neutral. "This was always going to be dangerous regardless of the weather, Rick. We'd understand if you changed your mind."

Rick stared into the pelting rain. "No. I'm in this to the end."

The door opened and George got back in the car, hair soaked and raindrops dripping off his nose and chin. "Geez, I think it's raining harder now than it was this morning." No one responded. He looked from face to face as he started the car. "What's going on? Are we having second thoughts?"

Julia answered, "No, Steve was just explaining to Rick the importance of leaving today. That's all."

The boy Lucy had dispatched to open the gate was waiting for them. George drove onto the ramp and pulled up to *Haley's Comet.* They all sat for a minute watching the rain drops dimple the puddles on the tarmac.

"Damn, I hate preflighting in the rain," said George.

"Not to mention that we're going to get soaked loading the supplies," added Julia.

"Well, it seems to have let up a little. We might as well get started."

By the time they finished transferring the supplies into the plane, the rain had settled down to a drizzle. Julia drove the car back to the rental office. Rick and Steve sorted and stowed the equipment. George saw to the fueling and completed the preflight. When they'd finished their respective tasks, they went to the office to wait for Julia to return by cab.

George called for another weather briefing from Flight Service. As he was hanging up, Lucy stepped into the lounge area. "Heading back home, George?" she inquired.

The question caught him by surprise. "Er...ah, yeah," he stammered.

"I see you picked up a couple of passengers."

"Oh, yeah...Lucy, this is Steve Raimus and Rick Vanbrough." Both men rose to greet Lucy. George paused for a moment to gather his thoughts, then continued, "Steve and Rick are friends of ours. They're hitching a ride back to Detroit."

Lucy smiled pleasantly to Steve and Rick, then turned back to George. "Where's Julia?"

"She's returning the rental car."

"Why didn't you say something? I could have had Greg follow her over and bring her back."

"Well, thanks Lucy, but it's no trouble for her to take a cab."

"I don't expect that it is, but I like to help out when I can."

"Thanks, I'll keep that in mind." George gave a smile that he hoped looked suitably grateful, even though he wished she'd just go.

Lucy showed no evidence of complying with that wish. "So, how's the weather look for the trip?"

"The ceiling is lifting. Should be okay by the time we leave."

"It was supposed to stop raining this morning." Lucy frowned. "Weather like this sure puts a crimp in my business."

"Well, maybe next weekend, eh?"

"Yes, there's always next weekend."

The small talk had grown thin and George was glad when saw Julia's cab pull into the parking lot. "Well, boys," he said to Steve and Rick, "Julia's back. Time to get going."

"Bye, Lucy," Steve said as he went out into the rain

"Nice to meet you," Rick added.

"Nice to meet you boys, too." Lucy turned to George. "I hope it wouldn't be another two months before I see you again."

George studied Lucy's kind, honest face. He hoped she'd never discover what was really going on. "Whenever it is, I'll look forward to it. See you later, Lucy."

"Say goodbye to that lovely wife of yours for me."

"Will do," George said as he pulled the door shut.

George waited while the others settled into the passenger compartment of *Haley's Comet*. "Everybody still okay with this?"

"Yeah, sure, George," answered Steve.

"Absolutely," added Rick.

"Well, this your last chance to back out. Once the wheels are up, I'm not turning back."

"We know," said Julia. "Let's get going."

"I just want to review everything one last time."

The other three sighed as one. George sighed, too. "Hey, I just want to make sure everybody knows what they are supposed to do. Things are gonna happen fast." He paused as they nodded their agreement. "Julia will stay up front and help with the landing," he continued. "As soon as we're down, Rick and Steve will jump out and stand guard while Julia and I secure the plane and prepare it for takeoff."

"Right," said Steve.

"Then we all swing the plane around. I'll lead the way to the camp. We know that Haley and Strand are being held in the guest house. Julia and Rick will work their way around the back of the building, and try to find a way in. You've got the prybar and cutters, right?"

"Yes, George," said Julia. "We managed to remember them."

George ignored her sarcastic tone. "Steve and I will distract the guards in the front, so Julia and Rick can hit them with the tranquilizer gun. Then we grab Haley and the Judge and head back to the plane."

"And if we can't get in the cabin..." Rick said.

Julia ended his sentence. "We notify George and Steve by radio, and move around to the front to cover them while they try it from the front."

"Right," said George. "But you'll only have about a few seconds once we rap on the front door, so whatever you do, make it quick. Speed and stealth are our only hope. If anything goes wrong—I mean anything—give up. We're seriously outgunned. If bullets start flying, somebody is going to get killed."

Rick leaned back in his seat. "What do you think the odds are of us pulling this off?"

George looked down at his hands. "Maybe fifty-fifty. It won't take much to alert somebody that something is going on."

There was a silence, broken by Steve. "Hey, we can do this."

"That's what you said about Highway 89," said Rick.

"Well, this isn't Highway 89. And if you and Bobby hadn't panicked, we could have pulled that one off too."

"We didn't panic! You're the one who—"

George cut across him. "Take it easy, guys." Then to Rick, "Steve's right, this isn't Highway 89. It's going to be dangerous, but if we are careful and quiet, we can do it." Then he headed to the cockpit with Julia, leaving Steve and Rick sitting in silence and staring at each other.

Chapter 18

The rain at Meigs Field had all but stopped as George advanced the throttles and *Haley's Comet* began the takeoff roll down runway 36. Once they'd reached five hundred feet, he banked to the right, out over Lake Michigan before leveling off at fifteen hundred feet, just below the cloud deck. Once clear of O'Hare's influence, he turned North, setting the course for Lake Ogoki.

Julia was in the right seat, staring out at gray clouds streaking past above and at gray water below. Droplets of rain beat on the windshield, but the slipstream guided them immediately up and back along the fuselage. Up ahead, George could see a lake freighter making its way toward the Sault locks.

Through the intercom, he said, "Julia, just in case anything goes wrong, you disappear into the woods. There's a road that ends on the south side of Melchett Lake, which is about ten miles south of Ogoki Lake. That road runs into Aroland. That's at the beginning of a minor highway. It's also a stop on the Canadian National Railway." He reached into his pocket, pulled out a small compass and offered it to her. "Just in case."

"Nothing will go wrong."

"Like I said, it's just in case."

Julia looked down at the military-style compass without accepting it. "That's the one Haley gave you, isn't it? For your first year anniversary."

George nodded. "Take it for me, okay?"

"For you." She took the compass and slipped it into a pocket on the sleeve of her jacket.

They droned on, straight up Lake Michigan but staying slightly closer to the Michigan side, avoiding the area of military restricted air space just off Sheboygan, Wisconsin. Once past the restricted area, George changed course slightly to the northwest, still flying below the cloud deck. He glanced down, noticing that the chop was still fairly heavy on the lake. Judging by the direction of the waves, they had to be bucking a pretty good head wind.

Soon he could make out Detroit Island, a beautiful wilderness marking the entrance into the Green Bay. Across Green Bay, they entered the mouth of Little Bay De Noc, just east of Escanaba. The cloud deck had risen appreciably, so George was able to gain a little altitude before crossing the beach on the west shore of the bay. Now heading inland, they crossed Highway 41, just west of two little towns situated on the north shore of Little Bay De Noc: Masonville, and Rapid River.

They ran nearly parallel to the highway for twenty-five miles, until the road veered to the Northwest, crossing their flight path for the last time on its eighteen hundred mile northern journey to the tip of the Keweenaw Peninsula. They crossed another highway between Sundell and Rumley, racing over the pines below. Soon, George could make out the vast expanse of Lake Superior through the marginal weather. He began to let down again, planning to cross the big water at no more than two hundred feet. All the while, he scanned the sky to the north and west for the trailing edge of the front.

They left the rugged, southern shore of the giant lake behind them, skimming over the waves. George needed to devote all his concentration to flying now; at this altitude, there could be no room for error. His imagination played out the horror of a crash into the icy waters, but he forced his brain away from such thoughts. He glanced over at Julia, who was gazing out with an expression of awe on her face.

"It's beautiful," she said.

"Cold, too."

"You ever fly this low before?"

George allowed a smile to creep over his face. "It's every pilot's dream, flying low and fast. It's dangerous but there's nothing like it." He checked the airspeed: holding steady at 220 knots.

"And all this time I thought you were the world's safest pilot."

He forced himself to look serious again. "I am. I really am. I wouldn't do this if it wasn't necessary."

A sailboat appeared in their path. George jinked slightly to the west so they wouldn't go directly over it, but the crew still gaped open mouthed to see the plane scream by at more than 200 knots. He hoped the sailors hadn't had time to note the aircraft numbers.

Twenty minutes later, the Canadian shore came into view. George planned on crossing Highway 17 between Schreiber and Terrace Bay. He was aware of a small airport off to their left, but that at this time of day and with marginal weather conditions, he didn't expect much activity. Just before they crossed the shoreline, he gained a hundred feet of altitude to allow for any unusually tall trees or power lines that weren't indicated on the charts.

As they flashed over Highway 17, only two cars were visible. George was sure that *Haley's Comet* would be out of sight before anyone even realized what had happened. They'd be over a sparsely populated forest area for the next fifty miles, until they crossed Highway 11, ten miles west of Geraldton. After that, it would be bush country all the way to Ogoki Lake.

He turned to Julia. "You'd better go back and see how Steve and Rick are doing. You should start getting ready, too."

"What about the weather?"

George strained his eyes toward the northwest. The sky was becoming lighter. "We may luck out yet. It looks like the back end of the cloud deck out there. At least the ceiling appears to lifting. If we can get higher before cutting power, there's less chance of anyone on the ground noticing us. That should give me plenty of time to set up for a dead stick landing."

Julia unfastened her seatbelt and started back toward the passenger compartment. George grabbed her arm and pulled her back toward him. He looked at her for long moment. "Are you sure you want to go through with this?"

"I'm sure." She bent down and kissed him. "You're not going to have all the fun without me."

He kissed her back. "We're going to be all right, Julia"

Her smile, more than his own confidence, assured him he was right. She kissed him again. "I know." Then she pulled away and continued toward the rear.

As Julia stepped through the curtain, Rick had already changed into his camouflage gear and was attempting to adjust his bulletproof vest. Steve was sitting and idly examining a pistol from the supplies, oblivious to her entrance.

Rick patted the vest. "Man, as heavy as this thing is, it ought to be able to stop a cruise missile."

"Let's hope you don't have to find out."

Steve started from his reverie. "Oh, Hi, Julia."

"Hi, Steve. Sorry if I disturbed you, but George thinks we ought to get ready."

Steve set the pistol down. "How close are we?"

"About thirty minutes or so, I'd guess."

"It still looks pretty crummy out there. Is George going to be able to pull this off?"

She gave a confident nod. "We need to gain altitude to maintain the element of surprise and to get some maneuvering room. We only get one shot at this, so George needs to line us up perfectly."

Steve stared for a few seconds without responding. Then he got up laboriously and went to the bag that held his things. Without another word, he began pulling things out to change into his camouflage clothes.

Julia shrugged, went to her own bag and started to do the same. When she slipped out of her blouse and slacks, Rick blushed and turned away, intent on applying insect repellent. Steve seemed unfazed, glancing at her occasionally—admiringly but not necessarily lecherously.

She was in the process of pulling on her pants when a sudden lurch made her fall against him. He grabbed her by the arms and held her up. Rick ducked his head away, noticing nothing.

With her pants still around her knees, Julia struggled to regain her footing. "I'm sorry, Steve." She could feel her cheeks burning.

Steve chuckled as he released her. "I'm not."

Rick chimed in, "This isn't exactly a great locker room, is it?"

Julia used the distraction to regain her composure, "It sure isn't. I wish we could have changed before we left, but it would have looked strange at the airport."

"No doubt," added Steve, who had returned to his seat and was lacing up his boots. He looked out the window. "The clouds are breaking up. I always said that George was a lucky bastard."

Julia buttoned up her shirt and started back to the front. They were ascending. She stopped before the curtain and turned to Rick. "Would you do me a favor and lay out George's things on one of those empty seats?"

"Sure thing," he answered, waving her off with the assurance that it would be taken care off.

She pressed his shoulder and passed back through the curtain.

"Hey, you look great. You should have joined the army," George said as Julia slipped back into the right hand seat.

"Yeah, olive drab always was my color."

"Everything okay back there?"

Julia hesitated, remembering the unintentionally intimate moment she'd shared with Steve. "Sure," she finally said. "How about up here? Where are we?"

"We crossed Highway 11 about five minutes ago."

She glanced outside. "Looks like it's clearing up."

"I told you the weather would cooperate."

"You are a lucky bastard, George."

"What?" he said, surprised by the statement.

"You heard me." She laughed, looking out the window. The sky above was brightening, but the lowering sun was casting longer shadows on the ground. "It'll be getting dark soon. Are you going to be able to find the airstrip?"

George reached into his bag and pulled out a handful of aerial photographs. "You can help." He handed the photographs to Julia.

She looked down at the first photo, then out the window again. The photo was small, the image of the airstrip tiny—and the wilderness below was vast. "George, how in the hell are we going to find this?"

"Don't worry, we've got another forty miles to go. Ogoki is a good sized lake. It won't be that difficult to spot. The strip is about a half-mile directly to the south."

They both watched the endless canopy of forest, punctuated by glittering lakes, as *Haley's Comet* continued to climb. Crossing the Canadian National Railway, they could just make out the town of Aroland to the east. To the west, the tracks receded into an endless wilderness. A few minutes later, George pointed out a narrow track that weaved out of the north. "That's the road from Melchett Lake to Aroland."

They gained more altitude. "Two more lakes up ahead," George said.

Julia bent over the photos. "The bigger lake to the north looks as though it might be Ogoki," she affirmed. "But I can't tell for sure until we get directly over it."

George leveled off and reduced power. "I'm sure that's it, Julia. The one directly below us is Melchett Lake."

Julia checked the photo again and nodded in agreement.

George reached back and pulled the curtain aside. "This is it, boys," he called. "Get your seatbelts on. And start praying."

George pulled the throttles back to idle and cut power. *Haley's Comet* began to descend. He trimmed for the appropriate glide angle and then turned to Julia. "Hold the wheel for a moment, okay?"

He pulled a pair of binoculars from his flight bag and scanned the forest up ahead, searching for the telltale slash in the trees that would indicate the location of the airstrip. He couldn't see any sign of it, and the lake was approaching rapidly...maybe it wasn't Ogoki Lake after all.

Then he saw a break in the trees. George lowered the glasses without changing the direction of his gaze. He lost it for a moment before locking on again.

It was the strip.

The lowering sun no longer illuminated the ground below the trees. The strip was a black gash in a sea of green. This was going to be the most difficult landing he'd ever made. He recovered the controls and squeezed Julia's hand.

She squeezed back. "You can do this, George."

He nodded. "No, sweat. Just make sure your seatbelt is extra tight, okay?"

Staying to the south of the lake, and of the hillock separating the airstrip from the cabins, he spiraled down to the left, keeping the airstrip just in front of them. At two thousand feet, the ground was coming up fast. He reduced the glide angle, bleeding off airspeed and trying to set up for a landing at the southeast end.

Fifteen hundred feet and the trees were filling the windscreen. He prayed he'd timed it right; there could be no second chance. Settling on a right-hand base leg, he aimed to be at a thousand feet when they turned on final. Watching the airspeed carefully, he banked onto their final approach.

"Hang on," he called as he lowered the gear and added flaps.

The end of the airstrip approached. They were still carrying too much speed. He couldn't afford to overshoot the threshold of a two thousand foot runway, so he induced a slip that would bleed off more airspeed.

Too much: they were going to be short. He retracted a few degrees of flaps and pulled the nose up slightly.

The airplane lurched as the gear brushed tree tops, but he managed to keep it under control. They cleared the last of the giant pines and sank into the darkness of the man-made clearing. The trees now towered on either side. George felt for the ground, unable to tell how straight they were heading.

The right main gear touched first, digging into the rain-soaked earth. *Haley's Comet* swung wildly in that direction as George fought to keep from ground looping into the forest. Then the left gear touched down, pulling them back around. George compensated by alternating the brakes. As he fishtailed down the strip, he took a moment to give thanks for the soft ground which was absorbing their speed voraciously.

Haley's Comet bounced to a stop. For several seconds, nobody said a word.

George looked around. "Everyone all right?"

"Yeah." Rick seemed to speak for all. "But I think I just camouflaged my underwear."

George shut down all the aircraft systems, unfastened his seatbelt, and, feeling his way in the semi-darkness, made his way to the rear, Julia right behind him.

Rick was gathering up his things, but Steve sat stonily, staring out the window. George placed his hand on Steve's shoulder and said, "See anything?"

Steve looked up, "No...no. Looks like you did great, man."

"Thanks," George said, and peeled off his soaking wet shirt. Within a few minutes, he was ready. "Everybody clear on what to do?" He paused while they answered in agreement. "Then, let's get going." He stuffed a 9mm into its holster and reached for the door latch.

The door opened to the gloom of the evening forest. George listened for a few seconds and then descended the three steps, searching the darkness for any movement. Nothing caught his eye, but something made him turn toward the tail of the plane.

"Buenas Noches, Little Wing."

Brady Keyes stepped out of the shadows. Tony Lopez and Juan Guterriez stood behind him, each holding an Uzi trained in George's general direction.

Chapter 19

"I knew you would miss me, but I must say that I'm flattered that you couldn't stay away more than a couple of days." Brady smiled thinly.

George clenched his teeth, fighting back the fear and anger that was threatening to overwhelm him. He had known what they had undertaken would be risky, but he had thought that they had at least a fair chance. Now, all was lost, and worse, Julia was back in danger.

What had possessed him to let her come?

"I see you're armed. Were you planning to shoot me?" Brady held out his hand for George's side arm.

Slowly, George pulled it out of the holster and handed it over to Brady. Then he heard Rick say something from inside the plane and he turned back toward the doorway, hoping to stop Rick or Steve from doing something stupid and getting them all killed. "It's over, guys. Come on out," he said quietly.

Rick stepped down first. "What's going on, George? We need to—" He spotted Brady and fell silent.

"Well if it ain't the Over the Hill Gang," Brady said.

Rick didn't move. "Speak for yourself, asshole."

"You don't seem happy to see me."

Julia emerged and stood next to George. Brady bowed slightly before her. "Mrs. Ashton. So nice to see you again."

George could tell she was fighting back tears as she turned

to him and said, "You did so well. I can't believe they saw us coming."

Brady chimed in. "Wasn't it great? Dead stick landing on a grass strip in the middle of the forest and damn near dark to boot! Can this guy fly or what?"

Steve had still not emerged from the plane. George was starting to get concerned that he might try to play the hero. He was relieved when Steve came through the doorway unarmed.

"Mr. Raimus. Good of you to come. It's just like old times, isn't it? Too bad Bobby is no longer in a position to join us," said Brady.

George frowned. How did Brady know that Bobby had died? He hadn't known himself until he first talked to Steve. Then he looked at Steve and it became clear.

"Cut the crap, Brady," Steve said. "This isn't pleasant for anyone."

"Not even you, my friend?"

"Especially not me."

Steve went over and stood beside Tony before turning back to George. "I'm sorry," he said.

"Why?" George couldn't think of what else to say. He was still reeling from the shock.

Steve said nothing, but Brady answered for him. "Why do you think?"

"You sold us out?" stammered Rick.

"It wasn't just the money," Steve replied.

"Mr. Raimus," Brady interjected, "is just being a loyal employee."

George glared at Steve, who was now just staring at the ground. "You were working with Brady? All that shit about wanting to help me..." He paused, trying to control his anger. "It must have been hard for you to keep from laughing all weekend." Suddenly George exploded. "You son of a bitch!" He lunged at Steve, but Julia grabbed his arm and pulled him back. Juan and Tony leveled their guns, and George became aware of two other men behind them, also pointing their weapons at him.

Brady cursed and slapped at the side of his neck. "These damn mosquitoes are eating me alive." He motioned to the gunmen. "Juan, bring Mrs. Ashton along. Tony and Ramone can take the others." He turned back to George. "I'm sure you've all had a long day and would like to get some rest, eh?"

✦

The guest house was brightly lit, and George could see his employer through one of the windows. Haley was sitting on a bed. He looked around as the jeeps pulled in to the camp.

Ramone jumped out from behind the wheel of the jeep and trained a weapon on the prisoners. Tony, sitting in the back, thrust his gun barrel into Rick's ribs. "*Vamonos.*"

George got out. Rick followed him. The two gunmen herded them toward the guest house.

The second jeep was parked near the main cabin. Brady and Juan were escorting Julia inside. George started towards her, but Ramone pushed him down the path leading to the guest house. George craned over his shoulder, trying to keep Julia in sight. Ramone shoved him harder.

"Get your goddamn hands off me," George said angrily, but he was now moving toward the door and the man seemed satisfied.

The cabin was open when they got there, and a young Latino was standing in the lighted threshold, an Uzi slung over his shoulder, his right hand clutching the grip. He and Ramone exchanged a few words in Spanish, and then laughed. Tony, who had been escorting Rick down the path, spoke more harshly and the youngster stepped aside to allow all four inside. Once in, he evidently asked for permission to leave, which Tony granted, so he let himself out and shut the door.

Standing, blinking in the relatively bright lights, George focused on Haley standing between the two beds. Judge Strand was lying on the bed closest to the window.

"Is that our pilot?" said the Judge weakly.

Haley didn't take his eyes off George. "Yes, Albert, it is."

Ramone gave George one last shove in Haley's direction. Tony followed suit with Rick. Standing almost face to face with Haley, George finally spoke, "Are you all right, sir?"

"What the hell do you care?"

"I didn't have any choice." George was painfully aware how lame that must sound.

"So, what did you come back for? More money?"

"I...we came back for you. And the Judge."

Haley looked at him suspiciously. "Why did you do all this?"

There was no point trying to explain, not now. It would be better to wait until the shock of the moment had passed and they would be able to speak more rationally. And George didn't want to mention Julia in front of Brady's men. "I know how it must seem right now, Mr. Haley, but I swear that I didn't do it willingly."

Haley glanced at Tony and Ramone, who were chattering in Spanish but still aiming their weapons in George's general direction. "Who's this?" He nodded toward Rick.

"This is Rick Vanbrough, Mr. Haley. He's a friend of mine. He came to help."

Rick held out his hand. Haley studied it as if checking for weapons, then accepted it.

"I'm sorry to have to meet you under these circumstances," Rick said.

Haley nodded curtly before withdrawing his hand, then turned his withering gaze back to George. There was a jangling sound as Tony tossed two pairs of handcuffs to Haley. "Ol' man, put these on the pilot and the fat one," he said in his heavily accented English. Then he motioned to the bed. "Cuff yourselves to the frames."

"What do you need these for?" George protested. "You've got the guns."

"Yeah, we got the guns." Tony waved his firearm as if to emphasize his point. "So you better do what I say."

Haley scooped up the cuffs and motioned to George to sit

on the floor at the end of the bed. A few seconds later, George's wrist was secured to the bed frame. Haley repeated the process with Rick, at the foot of the Judge's bed.

Tony came over and yanked on George's arm, assuring himself that the handcuffs were secure. The gunman wasn't gentle; George winced. Tony did the same to Rick, then said something to Ramone in his rapid-fire Spanish before leaving the cabin. Ramone pulled up a chair and sat down, glaring at the group of hostages. He set his Uzi on the wooden table, close to his left hand.

The cabin was silent for several minutes, disturbed only by the Judge's labored breathing. Eventually, Haley went over to him. "How are you doing, Albert?"

"Been better...but why is George here?"

Haley flicked an angry look toward George. "I mean to find out."

George avoided Haley's eyes, turning instead to Rick's florid face. The big man seemed in better shape than the Judge, but that wasn't saying much. Something about George's appraisal seemed to spook him. "What is it? What?"

"Nothing," George answered. "I just wish I'd never brought you in on this."

"I knew what the score was. You never minced any words about it." He paused, looking around the cabin, "We'll find a way out."

Without taking his eye's off Rick's face, George tilted his head slightly in Ramone's direction. He was fairly sure Ramone understood some English. Rick changed the subject immediately. "I can't believe that Steve was in on this. I swear, if I ever get my hands on that bastard..."

There had been too much happening for George to dwell on Steve's betrayal, but Rick's words rekindled the flame. Steve had played him for a fool. George himself had done the same to Haley, he thought, but that had been for Julia. Steve had done it for money.

He went back over the weekend. Steve had even gone so far as to collect supplies with Julia, knowing that they would be useless. He had to be laughing his ass off.

Or did he? Could there have been some other reason, beside money? There had been for George, when he turned Haley and the Judge over to Brady. Maybe they'd gotten to Steve somehow, too.

George shook his head and backed away from that line of thought. He couldn't allow his emotions to overrule logical thought just now. Too much was at stake.

Steve Raimus hadn't touched his beer. He sat across from Brady in the kitchen of the main cabin. Roy Lassiter leaned against the counter behind Brady, clutching a flask of whiskey.

Brady took a swig of beer and slammed the bottle down on the red checkered table cloth. "Fuck those idiots, Ray-man. What did they ever do for you?"

"They were my friends." Steve hung his head. "I know that doesn't mean much to you."

"Cut the violins. I tried to get George to play along. It would have been great to have him on board. But no, he had to be the hero." Brady shook his head disbelievingly. "And he brought his wife!"

"It was the only way he could see to do it."

"And all for two bourgeois pigs like the ones we were fighting back in the sixties. Why should he care about them now?"

Steve shrugged. "Haley gave him a job when he needed one. Helped him get established."

"Yeah, the es-tab-leesh-ment, that's what Brady's talking about, man," Roy commented.

Steve looked from one to the other. "I don't see you living the hippie lifestyle."

"We lost that fight." Brady took another swallow of beer. "All anybody thinks about is money anyway, so hell, now we're just playing their game."

"Except we play it better." Roy took a sip of his whiskey, and rolled it around his mouth before swallowing.

"Of course we do," Brady said. "Carlos Santez knows more about human nature than all the hippies put together." He fixed Steve with a dark stare. "He's taken good care of you, hasn't he?"

Steve wilted under the intensity of the other man's gaze. "Yes, Brady. He's taken good care of me."

"Damn straight, he has. Remember ten years ago when that insurance business of yours was failing? When you were skimming the premiums to keep the creditors off your back?"

There could be no snappy comeback to that, and Steve didn't even try to think of one. He just picked up his untouched bottle and took a sip of beer.

Brady continued, "It's payback time, Steve. That's why I called you when this was going down. I knew George might come to you. If he did, I had to get you to warn me."

Reluctantly, Steve nodded. He was in too deep. This was his world now, and these were his people. They'd rescued him from bankruptcy and offered him a profitable franchise as the main contact in Wisconsin for high-grade Colombian cocaine. The money Brady had waved in front of him made his head swim: more in the first month than he'd seen in the previous two years. It was an easy decision.

For ten years he'd lived the high life: a secluded mansion with German sports cars in the garage block and a membership at the country club—and a rejuvenated insurance business to front it all.

He took a long pull on his beer. It wasn't as if there was anything he could do. "George had the same chance I did. It's not my fault that he chose to be an asshole."

Brady smiled, clearly pleased.

That left one final piece of guilt for Steve to assuage. "Can you tell me what's going to happen to them?"

"If Hector is released and the cops don't get cute, Strand and Haley might just see their families again."

"What about the others?"

"Little Wing tried to fuck with me." Brady gave a regretful shrug. "He shouldn't have done that."

"And Rick?"

"Rick is a casualty of war."

"I just wish you hadn't told me to get him involved."

"George had to get backup from somewhere," Brady said. "Better you and Rick than the cops." He shrugged again. "Anyway, I never liked Rick."

Lassiter snorted with laughter. "The fat fucker just stepped on his own dick big time, that's all."

Brady laughed too, before turning back to Steve. "Don't worry, Ray-man. There's no need for you to be involved. You'll be safe at home and counting your money before anything ugly goes down."

Chapter 20

"You sure are the dumbest chick I ever met."

Julia ignored Naomi and kept staring out into the blackness of the night, through the same window from which she had watched George arriving with Haley and Strand the previous Friday. The room hadn't changed. It was as though the past two days had never existed.

She'd been back for two hours. Naomi had passed the time playing solitaire, taking brief time-outs to direct some more verbal abuse in Julia's direction, but Julia was too absorbed with her own dark thoughts to pay much attention.

"What the hell were you thinking about?" Naomi continued. "You had it made. You had your man back. You were Scott free. Why'd you go and screw it up by coming back here for them two old farts? Do you think they'd risk their necks to save you?"

Why wouldn't the woman just shut up and leave her in peace? Julia turned from the window and glared. "That's not how I decide to do things for people. I don't figure out what they might do in return."

"Bullshit, girl. Nobody does nothing 'less they gonna get something out of it."

"Maybe that's the way you people operate."

"That's the way everybody operates. Where you been?"

"I didn't just fall off the cabbage truck," Julia said. "This may be news to you, but not everybody puts their own interests first. George certainly doesn't."

"Then he's just as crazy as you. And he's sitting over there with them old guys right now to prove it."

"Those 'old guys' weren't getting out of here alive, were they?" Julia demanded.

Naomi said nothing.

"We were their only hope. I couldn't have lived with myself if I'd just walked away."

Naomi thought about it for a moment. "Well, there you go. You were getting something out of it: a clean conscience."

Confronted by such irrefutable logic, Julia had to smile. "If you're so smart, what are you doing hanging around with these losers?"

"What do you mean 'losers'? These boys got money liked you never dreamed. Damn, Roy spills more liquor in a month than your husband could buy in a year. And he takes good care of me too, you know what I mean."

"I know what you mean." Julia paused. "And I think you know what I mean, too. You don't need anybody to take care of you . You can take care of yourself . Roy just doesn't want you thinking that way."

"How do you know what I can or can't do?" Naomi sneered. "You can't even keep your own skinny ass out of trouble, so don't be telling me what's up and what's down."

"I'm just saying that you're a lot more capable than those bozos think you are."

"Yeah, right," Naomi said. "Why don't you just lay down and get some sleep. You're making me nervous, standing at that window all the time."

Julia knew that her whirling mind would no more permit sleep than Brady's goons would let her walk out the front door, but she was weary and lay down on the bed anyway. She'd just rest her eyes for a few moments...

Once the white woman was asleep, Naomi went to the kitchen to grab a sandwich. Julio was still on guard outside the door. She'd half expected to find Brady and maybe his friend Steve in the kitchen, but there was only Roy, sitting alone at the table with a row of empty beer bottles lined up in front of him and a half-full bottle in his hand.

At least he'd given up on the whiskey, for tonight. She'd probably be able to handle him now.

Roy looked up with bleary eyes. "What are you doing here, woman?"

"Getting something to eat, if it's any of your business."

"I thought you was supposed to be watching that bitch."

"She ain't going nowhere, 'less she gets past Julio."

"You better hope not, if you don't want your ass whupped."

Naomi turned toward him. "You can kiss my ass, Roy Lassiter."

Roy's chair skidded backward as he got to his feet. "Watch your mouth, woman. You keep talking like that, you're not gonna be able to talk at all."

Naomi stood her ground. "That's all you animals think about, shutting people up. Well, you can't stop me from talking."

"You're lucky Brady needs you in one piece." Roy subsided back into his chair.

"Well he does, and you'd better remember it."

"If it was me, I'd just shoot her and get it over with. It ain't like she's enjoying herself. What difference does a couple more days make?"

Naomi forced herself to hide her surprise. "So you're gonna shoot her?"

"Gonna do all three of them. The pilot, the skinny bitch, and the fat fucker. Ain't none of them any use to us."

Naomi tried to imagine why the three were still alive. She couldn't think of any reason, either. "Well, I guess Brady don't see things that way."

"Yeah. Maybe he wants to keep the pilot around for a while. Or maybe it's because he used to be friends with those two fuckers." Roy swigged his beer. "Or maybe he's gone soft in the head. We shoulda done them when they got off that plane."

Naomi opened the refrigerator and studied its contents with unseeing eyes, thinking about what Roy had said.

"Then we could get back to moving product," he continued. "This kidnapping ain't my thing. It ain't good business. Not like my regular work. Did I tell you how I opened up the Detroit market for Santez?"

Naomi sighed. "Only about a hundred times." She chose some cold cuts from the refrigerator and began to put together a sandwich.

"Yeah, well I never saw you do any business. I never saw you do anything except live the high life off me."

"You don't know what I do. You never bother to ask."

"Like I'd need to ask," Roy said. "I get the bills from all them fancy stores, remember?"

It was true: there wasn't much to Naomi's life except for spending Roy's money, and occasionally doing a job like this one, something that called for a woman's touch instead of a gunman's. She finished making her sandwich in silence, then slapped it on a plate, grabbed a beer, and headed for the door.

Roy caught her by the elbow as she passed, and spun her around so he could see her face. "It's okay, babe. That's why I make money: so you can look good." He released her arm and his hand shifted down to her thigh. His gaze shifted downward, too. "And you surely look good. Why don't you leave that sandwich for later? You and me can slide over to my room…"

She jerked away from him. "I got a job to do around here. Keeping an eye on that woman." She turned and marched to the door. As she left, she heard Roy's quiet laughter, and then a gurgle of beer.

Naomi sat on her bed, eating her sandwich as she watched Julia sleep. Naomi had known some good white people over the years; she certainly didn't hate them. But she didn't go out of her way to make friends with them either.

This particular white girl seemed like a decent sort, but you could never tell...sometimes they came on like they where your best friend, but then something would happen and the next thing you knew, you were getting the cold shoulder. Naomi couldn't tell where Julia was coming from, yet. She hadn't spent enough time with her, and now it looked like she never would. Suddenly, it didn't seem to matter that Julia was white.

When some of Roy's acquaintances had disappeared before, Naomi never gave it a thought. It was Roy's business: he took care of her, and she kept her nose out of his affairs. If anything happened to those people, well most likely they deserved it. Most of them were pushers or pimps or other such lowlifes. Some of them were killers themselves.

Julia was the first one Naomi had gotten to know, and the first one who hadn't done a single thing to deserve what was about to happen. Maybe she and her husband had caused some trouble for Roy and Brady, but they were just doing what they thought was the right thing.

But what could Naomi do about it, anyway? Nothing. What was going to happen, was going to happen whether she wanted it to or not. Besides, didn't Roy say that Brady might need to keep a pilot around? If they wanted George Ashton's cooperation, they sure wouldn't let anything happen to Julia. Maybe things would work our for her after all.

Naomi drained her beer, cleared the cards off her bed, and lay back. Roy had been a little rough on her sometimes, but he'd always taken good care of her too. She stayed in a beautiful condo, dressed in the latest fashions, and hung out in the best clubs. Considering where she came from, it wasn't such a bad a life. She reached over and flicked out the light.

Julia awoke from a fitful sleep. She lay quietly for a while, listening to the steady rhythm of Naomi's familiar snoring. Reassured that the other woman was deeply asleep, she sat up and looked around. The moon had risen over the pines and was now shining through the window, bathing the room in its pale light. Everything looked eerie and colorless. The only relief was the yellow pool of light spilling under the door that opened into the living room.

Julia studied the light, watching for shadows. Why had Brady given her preferential treatment by keeping her in this room with Naomi? He couldn't be concerned about her well being; he had nothing to gain by keeping her safe, unless he still had a use for George. That thought buoyed her spirits a little.

She climbed out of bed and crept to the door. Strain as she might, she couldn't hear anything. She tiptoed to the window, to where her jacket was hanging from the back of the chair. The compass George had given her was still in the sleeve pocket, and she gave silent thanks that the man who'd searched her had been more interested in a cheap thrill than in doing a thorough job. She retrieved the compass and cupped it in her hand, remembering George's words about disappearing into the forest if things went badly.

He could never have imagined that they'd wouldn't even make it off the plane without falling into Brady's hands. So, what good was the compass now?

Standing at the right edge of the window, she could just make out part of the guest house that stood off to the west end of the cabin. She couldn't see the front window, but light from the side window reflected off the pines growing nearby. Watching the branches sway in and out of the light, she considered the situation. Brady would never trust George, even if he had some use for him. Their current reprieve could only be a temporary one: it was clear to Julia what the final outcome must be.

If she ever wanted to see George again, she had to take matters into her own hands.

She had to escape.

The room blazed with sudden light, leaving Julia blinking in the glare. It was Naomi, sitting up in bed, her hand still resting on the switch. "Whatcha doing, girl?"

Julia searched for an answer. "I couldn't sleep. I was thinking about George."

Naomi's face softened. "Don't worry, I just talked to Roy a little while ago. George and his friend are okay."

The black woman actually sounded sympathetic. Was there a chance she might help? Julia gazed at her, willing it to be so.

Naomi stared back with a puzzled expression. "What's come over you, girl?"

Julia didn't reply. She wanted to ask for help...but she didn't dare to. If her instinct proved wrong, it could be disastrous.

A note of anger entered Naomi's voice. "What the hell you thinking about? What's come over you?"

Julia could stay silent no longer. "If you were in my place, wouldn't you want to get out of here?"

"Hell no! You try anything, you'll get your ass shot. They'd do it, as soon as look at you. Some of them think Brady's gone soft for keeping you around as it is."

Julia decided to take the plunge. "What about you? Do you think I ought to be shot?"

"Ain't up to me," Naomi said. "But it could be, if you don't shut up and get back in bed. Julio's sitting right outside, and I believe he'd allow me the use of his gun, if I asked him real nice."

"You know that's what's going to happen to us, don't you? You know we're going to be killed."

"I don't know nothing." Naomi folded her arms defiantly. "They don't tell me nothing."

"You said that Roy told you about George."

Caught in a contradiction, Naomi flushed. "Even if I did know anything, what makes you think I'd tell you? You ain't the boss of me."

"Of course I'm not. But I don't think you're a bad person, Naomi. I think you wish you didn't have to be part of this."

Naomi couldn't make her face or her voice deny that. "So what? I am part of this, and I got a job to do...which is to keep your skinny ass right here in this room."

"But you don't want anything to do with murder, do you?"

Naomi couldn't stand it any longer. "Look, girl. Ain't nothin' bad gonna happen to you or your man right now."

"Not right now, maybe, but they aren't going to keep us here forever."

"I don't know about that."

Julia decided to go for broke. "Would you help me if you did?"

"Shit, girl," Naomi snorted. "I wouldn't piss on you if you was on fire. Now, shut up and get back to bed."

Julia went to the bed and lay down. Naomi snapped off the light and they both lay in silence for a few minutes. Finally, Julia said quietly, "You'll tell me if you hear anything, won't you, Naomi?"

Naomi's answer told her what she wanted to hear. "Go to sleep, Julia."

Chapter 21

The pain in George's arm woke him up. As he lay quietly, trying to identify the source, other pains began to assert themselves in his back, neck and shoulder.

He was lying on a hard floor, propped against the wall with his arm hanging from a handcuff that was attached to the end of an iron bed frame. He managed to sit up a little straighter, bringing his body above his manacled hand. Blood rushed back to his arm, intensifying the pain. He groaned audibly.

"*Buenos dias,*" a voice said.

George turned his head painfully in the direction of the voice. It was Tony, sitting at the table and grinning at him. George rubbed his throbbing arm with his free hand, trying to gather his thoughts.

Tony flicked his eyes across the room. "The fat one, he looks dead." He laughed.

George glanced over at Rick. It was true, he didn't look well. His breath came in short shallow wheezes through his half-open mouth. Like George, he was manacled—he lay on the floor at the end of the other bed, propped up against the wall, his left arm dangling limply from a handcuff. George was hit by a pang of remorse. How could he have placed his old friend in this situation?

He turned back to Tony. "Are the handcuffs really necessary?"

"*Si.* You might sneak up on me, take my gun and shoot me." Tony laughed as he picked up his 9mm off the table and waved it in George's direction.

"Then forget about me. Just take them off my friend. He's not going to do anything."

"I don't think that is possible, Señor," said Tony, still grinning.

"Give it up, George," said a voice from the end of the room. "These bastards enjoy their jobs too much." It was Jack Haley, hidden by the end of the bed and out of George's view.

Gasping with pain, George pushed himself up until he could see Haley. The older man was still lying down, but had raised himself on his elbows.

"Good morning, sir. How are you feeling?" George said, still unsure of his status with Haley.

"I'm fine. I slept on a bed. How are you?"

"A little sore, but I'll live."

Rick's eyes fluttered open and focused on George. He stammered, "Mom? What's for breakfast?"

George managed to smile. "Good morning, dear. Better get up, or you'll be late for school."

Rick smiled lamely. "Jeez, Ma, you sure got ugly all of a sudden. Why'd you chain me to my bed like this?"

"Welcome to the S&M hotel," George said.

"Man, if this is what you get on your first night, what do they do if you don't pay your bill?"

"Let's not go there," George said. "Try sitting up a little straighter and rubbing your arm. It helps some."

The door opened and Ramone entered, followed by a breath of pine-scented air that did little to clear the smoke filled atmosphere of the cabin. Ramone turned to Tony and began a fast stream of Spanish, his Uzi dangling under his arm from its strap as he leaned on the table. Tony responded quietly, then reached into his shirt pocket and handed over a key. Ramone approached George and unlocked the handcuffs.

"You go with Ramone," Tony said in explanation.

"What for?"

Tony sighed. "Just do what the fuck he says."

Ramone stood back and motioned for George to get on his feet. George looked back and forth between the two, still not sure it was a good idea.

"You might as well go ahead, George," Haley said. "It won't make any difference."

The old habit of obeying his employer took over, and George pulled himself to his feet, groaning as he rose. As he stood facing Haley, he thought he detected forgiveness in the older man's eyes. Haley offered a slight smile. "It'll be all right."

Ramone poked the Uzi in George's side, prodding him toward the door. George turned to Ramone and pushed the gun away. "I'm going, asshole." He limped to the door and went outside.

In spite of everything that had happened, he was taken aback by the beauty of the place. A light mist lingered over the lake, shaded by tall pines as it waited for the sun to climb high enough to burn it off. The trees were alive with birds; calls of every kind blended together as each species strained to be heard above the din.

Then George became aware of a different sort of bird: the distant, distinctive *whump whump whump* of a helicopter. He paused between the guest house and the main cabin to listen more carefully. Ramone stopped too, cocking his head to the side. Within seconds, however, it became obvious that the sound was receding. Ramone frowned and nudged George toward the cabin again, steering him toward the back of the building.

Fear knotted George's stomach as they rounded the corner and Ramone pushed him toward a screen door. George opened it gingerly, and breathed a sigh of relief when he found himself in the familiar kitchen. Brady sat alone at the table, his elbows resting on the red and white checked tablecloth. He smiled thinly when he saw George.

"*Que pasa,* Little Wing? Did you have a pleasant night?" Brady motioned for Ramone to leave.

George suppressed the urge to leap over the table and grab Brady by the neck. It would have been pointless: even if he managed to take Brady, Ramone and the other gunmen were close by. "What do you think? Have you tried sleeping on a floor with your arm handcuffed to the end of a bed?"

"You'd be surprised at some of the conditions I've had to sleep in, but anyway, I'm sorry for the inconvenience. The boys were worried that someone might decide to get cute, and that there'd be too many of you to handle. Anyway, what's a few aches and pains? They prove you're still alive."

George considered the matter. "Will I still be suffering them tomorrow morning?"

Brady gazed out the window for a moment, then turned back to George. "That depends."

"On what?"

"On how the negotiations go."

"And how's that?"

"Our people in Colombia notified the US of the situation this morning. We are waiting for their response."

"How long will that take?" George wondered how Brady would communicate with the authorities without betraying his location. For that matter, how was he communicating with his people in Colombia?

"They have twenty-four hours to respond."

"I thought the US wouldn't negotiate with terrorists."

Brady's frown betrayed his displeasure at that label. "We're not terrorists. We are businessmen. And we know how the US government operates. They're businessmen, too. They can be quite flexible, as long as the press isn't involved."

George recalled the helicopter he'd heard earlier and wondered if the US was treating this like a business deal. He was sure it was a military helo, and he doubted if it was on routine maneuvers. "What happens if they don't like the price?"

"Carlos Santez is a smart businessman, and he hedges his bets. He has friends all over the world. One in particular has been causing ripples in the Middle East...I think you know who we are talking about." Brady smiled knowingly. "Believe me, the United States doesn't want anything to happen that would upset that delicate little apple cart. They won't like the price, but they'll pay it all the same."

George blanched. What had he gotten into? Could Brady really be playing in some international league of thugs, or was this just bravado to pump up the man's deluded sense of self-importance? Either way, George couldn't afford to challenge Brady's story. The best thing would be to go along with it. "What does all this mean to us?"

"If the US accepts our terms, then we will provide the authorities with the coordinates where they can find Strand and Haley—after, of course, Carlos has evacuated his business associates from the area."

"And the rest of us? Julia and Rick and me?"

Brady gave a regretful shrug. "There was no reason for you to be included in the deal. You chose to disregard my generous offer. I'm afraid that wasn't a very smart thing to do."

George swallowed hard, but kept calm. "Yet you're still keeping us alive. Why not just kill us and be done with it?"

"As I said, a good businessman hedges his bets. I wasn't planning on you being here, but your airplane represents an asset that might prove useful to me."

"What if I told you that I've had a change of heart? That I want to throw in with you and Santez?"

Brady laughed. "You had your chance for that." Then he became serious. "But tell me, why didn't you take it? What made you think you could get away with double crossing me?"

"Twenty-five years ago, we made a mistake," George said. "We've been paying for it ever since. I wasn't about to do it again."

"But you have, my friend. Except this time, you've spread the joy even further. How do you rationalize that?"

"I thought that Rick and Steve were like me. I thought they wanted a chance to make up for what they did. I didn't hide the risks from them."

"That I can understand," Brady said. "What I can't understand is that you involved Julia."

"I never wanted her to come. She insisted. I'd already betrayed her, and she made it seem as though I'd have betrayed her all over again, if I did this without her." George paused. "She made me feel like I could win."

Brady's smile was cold. "Really."

"Let her go, Brady. Rick, too. Do what you have to with me, but let them go. They can't harm you now."

"I wish I could," Brady said. "If it was just me, I would. But it's gone beyond that. You're in way over your head, now. Nobody fucks with Carlos Santez. Nobody."

"Brady, they don't know Santez from a pile of rocks. I'm begging you to let them go."

Brady's eyes became hard as flint. "You should have thought about the consequences before you decided to become a hero." He turned toward the door to the living room. "Ramone!"

Ramone entered the room. "*Si?*"

Brady spat a few words in rapid Spanish. Ramone nodded, grabbed George by the arm, and steered him toward the door. George pulled free and turned back to Brady. "You have turned into everything you fought against."

"You were the one doing any fighting, Little Wing. I was just in it for the good times."

George stared at Brady for a few seconds, then turned and left with Ramone.

Naomi was just about to enter the kitchen when the door burst open. The pilot, Julia's husband, stumbled out, followed by Ramone. Naomi stood aside to let them pass. Before she could continue through into the kitchen, she heard the inner door opening, followed by Roy's voice: "Word just came through that the Feds are about to give in."

She hung back, curious to hear more. Once she showed her face inside, the men would clam up.

"Carlos is one cool customer," Brady said. "I had my doubts about this mission, but he told me that if we did our part, he'd get his way, and so he has."

"So, do we finally get to dust the flyboy and his friends?"

"As soon as we're sure everything's going to plan. Until then, I feel more comfortable having an airplane and a pilot on hand."

Roy grunted. "The boys want to know if they can have some fun with the woman." He paused, but no answer came, and he continued in a conciliatory tone, "I told them I'd mention it to you, that's all. Don't worry, nobody'll touch her unless you give the high sign."

Naomi had heard enough. She pushed the door open and marched into the kitchen.

Roy gaped in surprise. "What the hell you doing here, woman?"

"I was just looking for a beer."

"Well, get out of my way." He shoved past her.

She looked at the refrigerator, then at Brady. "If that's all right with you?"

Brady just stood there, examining her like some bug. She stood her ground. "Do you mind if I get a beer?"

"Go right ahead."

She went to the refrigerator and pulled out a frosted bottle. All the while, she could feel Brady's cold eyes crawling over her skin.

Chapter 22

Julia was lying in bed, staring blankly at the ceiling. Naomi returned, crossing the room to sit in the chair near the window, but Julia ignored her. Other, tiny details had suddenly become more interesting to her, like the way the morning sun was breaking over the tall pines, and casting dancing branch shadows around the room. She looked past Naomi and out of the window. Two of Brady's men were standing near the little dock, chatting as they surveyed the shimmering water. They seemed incongruous against the picturesque setting, smart in their creased slacks and long-sleeve shirts and Italian shoes, with their Uzis cradled under their arms.

Naomi seemed…different. Ill at ease. She glanced at Julia, then looked away. Then she looked back.

"What is it?" Julia asked.

"Nothing. It ain't nothing." Naomi gazed out of the window for a while. Eventually, she turned back to Julia. "Why'd you go and come back here?"

"Naomi, we've been through this. What do you want me to say?"

"Nothing. I don't want you to say a goddamn thing."

Julia's curiosity was aroused, now. "Then what?"

"I just wish you had never come back here, that's all."

"Well, me too. But that's not the way it is."

A crafty look came over Naomi's face. "Supposing that it is the way it is. Supposing that you weren't here."

Julia studied Naomi carefully. "What are you saying?"

Naomi lowered her voice. "I'm saying you better start thinking about getting your skinny little ass out of here."

"But last time you said—"

"You better start thinking about it, real serious."

Julia was wide-eyed. "What do you know, Naomi?"

"I know you got to your ass out of this place."

Julia looked around, at the locked window and the guarded door. "But how?"

Naomi leaned forward and lowered her voice. "Maybe you can't do it by yourself. Maybe you need some help."

Julia scooted toward the end of the bed so she could be closer to Naomi. "You're going to help me?"

Naomi winced and glanced toward the door. "You deaf, girl? That's what I said, wasn't it?"

"But why?"

"'Cause it ain't right what those assholes are planning, and I'm sick of their shit."

Julia's eyes narrowed. "What are they planning? Is George all right?"

"Your husband's fine," Naomi answered. "For now, anyway."

"Naomi, what are they planning?"

Naomi squirmed in her chair.

"They're going to kill us, aren't they?"

Slowly, Naomi nodded.

Julia stood up and went to the door. Then she returned to Naomi. She'd never felt so helpless. Finally, she sat down again. Tears welled up but she fought them back; she wasn't going to cry. She was the one who'd insisted on coming along. She'd known the risk.

Julia didn't want that risk, or her presence on the mission, to have been for nothing. She was going to help get them out of it.

She looked at Naomi, so choked with emotion so it was hard to get the word out: "When?"

"I don't know, exactly."

Julia realized she was trembling. "I can't let you get mixed up this. You know what they'll do if they catch you. Just tell me when the best time to try is, and I'll tie you up before I go."

Naomi laughed. "You wouldn't make it, girl."

Julia stared into Naomi's eyes and understood that the woman was right. With Naomi's help, there might be a slim chance. Without it, there could be none. She nodded. "You're right. I wouldn't get far without you. But if you got caught helping me...well, I couldn't live with that."

Naomi grinned. "Girl, if we get caught, you won't need to."

Julia couldn't help smiling.

Naomi smiled, too, and for the first time since they'd met there was some real warmth in it. "You know, I ain't just doing it for you. It's for myself, know what I mean?"

Julia nodded.

Naomi paused and looked at the ground. "I just hang with Roy 'cause...well, you know. Mostly I ain't worried about the things he does. Thing is, it's been different since you been around. You ain't like the usual trash he gets mixed up with. You're...well, you're a lady. You ain't done nothing to deserve this."

Julia reached over and placed her hand on Naomi's. Naomi pulled away quickly. "Now, don't be getting gushy on me, girl," she said. "I told you, I'm doing this because I want to. Because I need to."

Julia withdrew into her own space. "I understand, Naomi. But I'm grateful all the same."

"Yeah, well, whatever." Naomi stood up and faced the window. "We got some planning to do, so let's get to it."

Naomi rapped gently on the bedroom door. "Julio?" Her voice was little more than a whisper. There was no response. "Julio?" This time she called a little louder, and feet shuffled outside the door. The door handle turned and Naomi stepped back.

The door opened a crack and a dark eye peered in. A voice said in very broken English, "Julio is not here. What the hell do you want?"

Naomi recognized the voice: it was Juan Guterriez, Tony's young cousin. This was going to be more difficult than she'd thought. "When is Julio coming back?"

"How the hell do I know?" Juan's voice was contemptuous. "What do you care?"

Naomi pressed on. "Because it gets lonely with nothing but this white girl for company, you know what I mean?"

Juan opened the door a little wider, looking her up an down as if seeing her for the first time. "How come you tell me this?"

"Because I need a man right now, and I thought you was one."

"You're Roy's woman. Go see him."

"I'm pissed off at that jerk. Besides, a girl likes to sample other chocolates in the box." She gazed at him admiringly. "And you look like an interesting one."

Juan ran his hand through his hair and looked around the deserted living room. It was late and everyone was either sleeping or on guard duty outside. He looked back at Naomi and smiled. "You think so?" Then he looked past her into the bedroom. "What about the woman?"

"She's asleep. If she wakes up, we'll let her watch." Naomi offered her most alluring smile. "And who knows, maybe she'll want to join in."

This was evidently more than Juan could resist. He took one last look around and then stepped across the threshold.

With the second step he took, there was a crunching sound and he went down like a sack of potatoes.

✦

Julia was shaking from head to foot, the brass lamp stand still in her hands. Looking down at Juan's crumpled form, she began to feel nauseous.

"Damn, girl!" Naomi said. "You surely did that sorry sucker in."

"You think I killed him?"

Naomi knelt down and put her hand on Juan's back. "He's still breathing. But he's gonna have a whopping headache when he wakes up." She rose and took the lamp from Julia, and set it on the bed. "We got to move him out from the doorway."

Julia took Juan's shoulders. He was too much of a dead weight for her to move alone, but when Naomi grabbed his ankles they managed to yank him away from the door. Julia shut it and then watched as Naomi tied his hands with the lamp's electrical cord.

"What if he calls for help?"

Naomi produced a roll of surgical tape and tossed it over. "I got this earlier, from the first-aid kit."

Julia gagged the unconscious man while Naomi finished trussing him. Then they slid him under the nearest bed—but not before Naomi had removed the handgun from his shoulder holster.

Julia asked, "Do you know how to use that?"

"Sure. You point it and pull the trigger."

Julia arched an eyebrow. Naomi chuckled and shoved the gun in her belt.

They slipped on their jackets and stood by the door, listening. There was no noise from the living room. Naomi eased the door open, looked around, and then stepped through. She motioned for Julia to follow. The only illumination came from a lamp on a small table, close to the bedroom door. A scantily-clad Playboy model gazed up from a double-spread on the floor, grinning vacuously.

They crept across the room. Naomi paused and pressed her ear to the door of the other bedroom. She nodded to Julia and smiled, pantomiming sleep with her hands clasped together at her cheek. Julia continued to the front door and peeked through the window curtains, waiting for Naomi to join her.

It took a while for her eyes to grow accustomed to the dark.

When they did, she saw one of Brady's men passing by, right outside the front porch. She shrank back, gesturing to Naomi to do the same. Then she brushed the curtain aside again. This time, she saw nothing. She nodded to Naomi, who turned the knob slowly and opened the door.

The hinges squeaked and Julia winced with fear—but the door was open enough for them to slip through. Then Naomi opened the screen door and the rusty chorus was renewed. They moved out to the porch, Julia closing the doors as gently as she could. They waited to determine if anyone had heard. The moon was rising over the pines, helping them to see, but also making them more visible to others.

They tiptoed down the wooden steps, stepping gingerly to avoid any more noise. They continued across the front lawn, around the side of the house and onto the two track that led into the woods toward the airstrip. The guards could be anywhere, Julia knew. She looked from side to side, straining to make out any hint of a human figure. Beside her, Naomi did the same.

At last they merged into the shadows of the forest that arched over the road fifty yards behind the main house, and Julia breathed a little easier for a couple of seconds—until voices cut through the night, speaking in Spanish. Whomever it was, they were coming closer. Julia grabbed Naomi's arm and pulled her off the road, praying that the wind in the trees, and the chirping of the crickets, would help to mask the noise of her panicked motion.

They huddled behind a huge pine. Two men passed by, returning from the airstrip. They must be patrolling, Julia realized. The men were plainly visible in the moonlight—which meant that Julia and Naomi would be, too.

As soon as they were out of earshot, the two women stepped back onto the road and continued toward the airstrip. Ten minutes later they stood in the shadows looking out onto the strip. *Haley's Comet* sat at the other end, covered by a large canopy of camouflage netting.

"I sure hope you know how to use the radio in that thing," Naomi whispered. "I'm not crazy about hanging around while you figure things out. There's no telling when another bunch of those goons are gonna show up."

"I won't be long," Julia said. "Just keep an eye out while I'm inside." She pulled Naomi along behind her, working her way along the edge of the forest toward the plane.

They moved around the tail, past the weird lunar shadows cast by the camouflage netting and toward the door on the port side. Julia reached up and jerked the handle, pulling the door open and revealing the three small steps up into the darkened cabin.

She turned to Naomi. "Wait here and watch for trouble." Then she reached into the sleeve pocket of her jacket and pulled out George's compass. "Here," she said, handing it to Naomi. "If anything happens, don't worry about me. You just head for the forest and just keep going south until you reach the road."

Naomi scrutinized the compass as if it were the first one she'd ever seen. It probably was, Julia realized. "It's easy," she explained. "Just flip up the lid, hold it level and wait for the rosette to stop turning." She coached Naomi through the process. "When it steadies, the arrow's pointing North. You head in the opposite direction. That's all there is to it."

"I guess I skipped this part when I was at girl scout camp." Naomi laughed. "Don't worry, I got it. Now, you get going so we can get the hell out of here."

Julia turned and climbed into the airplane. The passenger compartment was almost pitch black, so she had to feel her way up and into the cockpit. There, a little light filtered through the windows, but not much. She slid into the left seat and squinted at the instrument panel, which was nothing more than a dark hole. How was she going to find the master switch? She groped in the general area where she hoped it was, and pressed a rocker switch.

Nothing. She found another switch and tried that one, and the cockpit flooded with flashing red light. Startled, she looked outside. The light was reflecting off the camouflage tenting. It had to be scattering in all directions. Naomi was gaping up from below, strobe-lit and mouthing something unintelligible as she thumped the fuselage beneath the cockpit window.

Julia's panicked fingers fumbled for the source of the problem. Then it dawned on her: she'd found the master switch all right, but the switch for the beacon light on the tip of the vertical stabilizer had been left on. That light had activated when she pressed the master. She located the switch for the beacon, and flipped it off. The flashing stopped, but thankfully the panel instruments remained back-lit.

She glanced down at Naomi, now a dark shadow that was shaking its head disapprovingly. "Sorry, about that," Julia mouthed, hoping that the other woman would be able to lip-read by the faint light of the instrument panel.

She checked the road from which they'd just come, straining to see if anyone had been alerted by the flashing red light, and praying that the canopy over them had blocked most of the light.

George had left the headset draped over the control wheel. Julia pulled it on. The speakers were silent. She stared at the radio stack, trying to remember how to turn on the communications radio. She fingered the switches tentatively, and then took a chance with one. The speakers in the headset sprang to life.

"Ah, Toronto Center, United 646 requesting altitude change to flight level two niner zero," a practiced voice drawled.

It was an airliner high over head. Maybe she could get a message to that pilot.

"Toronto Center, United 646, roger that. Will report at two niner zero."

Julia fumbled for the microphone switch. She hit a button on the control wheel. "United airliner calling Toronto. This is 0418 Sierra, do you read me?"

Nothing. She waited for a few more seconds and tried again. "Airliner calling Toronto. This is 0418 Sierra, can you hear me?"

Maybe she didn't have the right switch. She located another one and pressed it. "United airliner calling Toronto, this is King Air 0418 Sierra. Do you copy?"

A few seconds later, she heard, "King Air 0418 Sierra, United 646 with you. What is your position?"

Tears welled up in her eyes at the sound of the friendly voice. "United 646, 0418 Sierra, we have a mayday situation."

"Roger that, 18 Sierra. What is your position?"

"We are on the ground, near a lake in Northern Ontario." She couldn't remember the name of the lake!

"Is any one injured, 18 Sierra?"

"No, we didn't crash. We were in a rescue operation for US Judge Albert Strand." It sounded so lame, but Julia hoped that the story of the missing Judge might have made it into the news.

There was a long pause, then, "18 Sierra, please advise position."

Julia fought down panic. There had to be ten thousand lakes in Northern Ontario. Without the name of this one, the radio contact would be useless. What was the name of the damn lake? She closed her eyes and visualized the map she had gone over with George so many times. There it was! "United 646, we are at a small strip, just south of Lake Ogoki."

"Roger that. Please advise the nature of your mayday." The voice sounded more skeptical than before.

The thumping resumed on the side of the plane. Julia looked down and saw Naomi gesturing wildly toward the woods. She followed Naomi's pointing arm and her heart froze. Lights, filtering through the trees, were moving toward the strip. A jeep was coming.

She mashed the microphone switch. "United 646, must terminate transmission. Please alert authorities." Without waiting for a reply, she tore off the headset, flipped the master switch, jumped out of the seat and ran toward the rear of the plane.

As she came to the door, Naomi grabbed her and urged her through. "They're coming!"

"I saw." Julia turned back to shut the door.

"Forget that shit!"

"If they see the door open, they'll know we were here. They'll know where to start searching."

Naomi nodded and helped her push up the steps. Their hands touched: Naomi was trembling. They closed the door and turned to sprint across the twenty yards of open ground to the woods. Julia saw the beam of a powerful flashlight sweep across the woods to their right. She pushed Naomi onto the ground and threw herself down beside her. The beam swept over their heads and picked out the airplane.

She whispered in Naomi's ear. "Get up and run, but stay low."

Naomi was already on all fours, moving in a rapid crawl that launched itself into a crouching run. Julia forced herself to leave the relative safety of being on the ground and made for the woods, closing the gap with Naomi so that they hit the tree line at the same time. She grabbed Naomi's arm. "Be careful were you step," she whispered.

The women slipped into the cover of the underbrush as the jeep reached the plane. They hid themselves behind a huge pine and peeked back through the undergrowth. Roy's voice sounded clearly, cutting across the sound of crickets.

"Look inside," he yelled.

One of the men opened the airplane door and stepped inside. Through the windows, they could see the beam of his flashlight bouncing around the interior of the plane. Roy stood in the headlights of the jeep with the other men.

The man who had gone in emerged, shaking his head. "Nada."

"Those bitches are around here somewhere." Roy looked around at the forest. When his eyes crossed the spot where Julia and Naomi were hiding he paused. Julia's heart was beating so hard she was sure he could hear it. Finally, he turned to the man standing next to him. "Gimme that." He grabbed the flashlight and played the beam around the woods. Naomi and Julia pulled back so they were completely hidden by the big pine. In spite of the chilly night air, Julia felt drops of sweat roll down her back as the light reflected off the trees near them.

"Look for tracks," Roy ordered. He moved slowly away from the plane, sweeping the flashlight over the ground in front of him.

One of the men reached into the jeep and pulled out another flashlight. He started to examine the ground behind the plane. The others shrugged their shoulders and followed suit.

They could hardly fail to find footprints in the soft grass. Julia picked up a pinecone and threw it as far to her left as she could. It sailed a good fifty feet before hitting a tree. Within a few seconds, four flashlight beams were converging on the spot.

"That's gotta be them!" Roy went crashing into the woods after the sound. The others followed.

Julia whispered in Naomi's ear. "This way." She gestured to the right. They threaded their way for about a hundred yards, and then she turned and started deeper into the woods. The sounds of the men faded. After about a quarter of a mile, the ground began rising: they had come to the small ridge that ran along the south side of the airstrip. At the top, they stopped to catch their breath.

Back at the airstrip, they could just make out the jeep's headlights reflecting off *Haley's Comet,* but there was no sound of pursuit.

Naomi's breathing slowed down a little. "Damn, that was way too close for me, girl."

"I thought they had us for sure," said Julia. "Are you okay?"

"Well, I could use a shot of bourbon, but I'll live." Naomi answered. "Did you get that radio figured out?"

Julia nodded. "I made contact with an airliner, but I don't know if he understood. Even if he understood, I don't think he believed me."

"Did you tell him where we are?"

"Yeah. I just hope he caught it."

"So, now what?"

"We have to get to George and the others."

"Now? Are you crazy girl? With all those idiots running around?"

"It's risky, but so is waiting. We don't know when..." Julia's voice trailed off.

Naomi put her hands on Julia's shoulders. "I understand how you feel, girl. But if we get caught, we ain't gonna be no good to no one."

The most important thing for Julia was to get to George, but she knew that Naomi was right. Roy and his men were kicking up dust everywhere between here and the guesthouse. If the women moved back to the camp now, they'd be caught for sure.

"All right," she finally said. "We'll wait for things to settle down."

Chapter 23

Jerry Kohler, assistant logistics supervisor at the FBI headquarters at Quantico, Virginia, chewed the last bite of his donut and washed it down with a slug of lukewarm coffee. He wiped his mouth and regarded the document on his desk. It was covered with powdered sugar. He brushed it away, smearing donut remnants across the numbers on the paper.

"Damn." He crumpled the paper and tossed it. "Marcie, would you run off another copy of the Operations Budget for me?"

At her desk outside the office door, Marcie rolled her eyes. "I just gave you one, Jerry," she said, barely concealing her contempt.

"And I need another one . Today, if you don't mind."

She said something he couldn't quite make out. Rachel McDonald, who sat mirror imaged outside another office, snorted with laughter as Marcy made her way to the copy machine.

Jerry craned his neck, watching Marcy as she walked away. Damn, that girl had a body, he thought, but what a bitch. He leaned back in his seat and sighed.

Bud Cowan walked in, looking back over his shoulder to catch the view. He almost bumped his head on the doorjamb.

Jerry looked up. "Jesus, Bud. You trying to get killed?"

"What?" A sheepish look came over Bud's face. "I didn't get hurt."

"I'm not talking about your noggin. If Marcie catches you ogling her like that she's going to kick your ass. She'll probably file a harassment suit, too."

"You're just pissed 'cause I got in your line of vision, you letch."

"It's your life. What's up?" Jerry could always count on Bud to keep him up to date on office politics.

"Didn't you hear?"

"Hear what?"

"The brass is going crazy upstairs. Seems they've located that judge the Colombians kidnapped from Detroit."

"No shit?"

"No shit. Seems the Colombians have him on ice somewhere in Northern Ontario."

"Ontario?"

"Yeah, it's in Canada—"

"I know where the hell Ontario is. How'd they find him?"

"No idea. But they're mounting a full scale operation. Marines, Mounties, Air Force, the works."

"Really?"

"Really. How about that?"

Bud always wanted recognition when he came up with tidbits, but Jerry wanted to be certain of the facts. "You sure about all this?"

"Of course I'm sure. Dave Hallet in field ops called me to cancel lunch today. They're jumping through hoops up there." Bud seemed a little crestfallen. "Ain't that something?"

"Well I'll be damned." Jerry stroked his chin thoughtfully.

"So, you free?" asked Bud.

"Huh?"

"For lunch. I'm looking for some company."

"Sorry, no can do. I've got to get the budget report updated today, or Langlois will have my ass."

"Yeah, right. You just want to moon around Marcie. You can't fool me, you dirty old man."

"'Course I can't. You're just way too sharp for me, Bud."

"Yeah, well, I'm going to see if Fred or Gil want to eat."

"Okay. See you later."

Bud paused in the doorway on his way out. "We'll be at the Roseland, if you change your mind."

"Sure thing. Thanks."

As soon Jerry was alone, he jumped up to shut his door. Back at his desk, he picked up the phone just as Marcie came in with a fresh copy of the Operations Budget.

Jerry slammed the handset down. "Jesus, Marcie, how many times have I told you to knock?"

"I thought you were hot for this." She tossed the document on his desk.

Jerry blushed slightly. "Oh, yeah, right. But please knock next time, will you?"

"You're the boss, Jerry." Marcie turned quickly, tossing her long hair as she withdrew from the office. She shut the door a bit too hard.

Damn, what a body, Jerry thought again. He picked up the phone and dialed.

"Jose? It's Jerry," he said in a low voice.

The line stayed silent.

"Jerry Kohler," he went on.

"Jerry who?"

Jerry struggled to keep the frustration from his voice. "Kohler. K...O...H...L...E...R."

"Ah. Kohler," the voice replied. "What have you got for us?"

Now that he'd established his identity, Jerry felt more settled. "Listen, this is big..." He repeated the story that Bud Cowan had just told him.

When he was done talking, he hung up the phone and gave a satisfied smile. It wouldn't be much longer now: two more years, and he'd have enough squirreled away to blow this pop stand.

Jerry Kohler would never had gotten by on the fifty-eight thousand the bureau paid him, not without the occasional bonus from Carlos Santez.

Chapter 24

George woke to the sound of someone banging on the door. "Ramone! Ramone!" There was more hammering. "Ramone!"

"*Si, si.*" Ramone raised his head from his arms and looked around blearily. The headlights of one of the jeeps poured in through the front window, casting harsh shadows around the room. Whoever was at the door started hammering again.

Ramone stood up, rubbed his eyes, and shuffled over to unlock and open the door. George couldn't see who was on the other side, but he heard a steady stream of Spanish, punctuated by an occasional question from Ramone.

Two days of exposure, and some determined dredging of memories, had brought back a little of George's high school Spanish, and he could now pick up bits and pieces of conversations. The current talk was going too fast for him to follow; the men were clearly agitated. One phrase was repeated enough for him to make it out: '*Las Señoras*'.

"What the hell is going on?" said Rick from across the floor.

"I don't know. Can't see anything." George strained against the handcuff that tethered him to the bed frame, trying to see around the open door.

Haley was sitting on the edge of his bed and shielding eyes from the glare of the headlights. "There's three men sitting in that jeep out there."

Ramone came back into the room and scooped up his gun from the table. The other man—Pablo, a youngster who acted as gofer to the others—trailed behind him. Ramone said a few more words and went back outside, closing the door behind him. Pablo stood by the table, surveying the room and looking both nervous and proud at the responsibility he'd been given.

The headlights retreated, then swung across the room and disappeared. The engine noise faded as the jeep headed down the road toward the airstrip.

Now that the young Pablo had been left alone with them, George thought he might be able to get some information. "What is going on?" he asked.

"The two Señoras gone away." Pablo's English seemed much better than the others'.

"What? Two women? Who?" George tried to stand.

Pablo patted the Beretta in his shoulder holster. "Sit down, Señor."

George subsided back to the floor. Could it be Julia? Who else could it be? "When did they escape?"

"In the dark," Pablo offered, shrugging his shoulders. "But will not get far."

"How did they get away?"

Pablo was beginning to get irritated. "None of your fucking business," he snapped. Then he sat down and began to thumb through a magazine from the table.

"Relax, George," Haley said. "He doesn't know anything."

"But Julia could be out there somewhere."

"Then she's better off than us," Rick said. "She's a resourceful lady, George. She'll be all right."

George ran his free hand through his hair. When he'd told Julia how to get to safety if things went wrong, he'd never meant for her to try escaping from an armed guard. "What could she have been thinking?" he moaned.

"At a guess: that somebody had to do something," said Rick. "She probably figured she was in a better position to do it."

"Didn't he say *'Señoras'?*" asked Haley.

"Yeah," said Rick. "I wonder what he meant by that."

"I don't know." George looked at Pablo, who was still leafing through the magazine. He decided to try for more information. "Pablo, you said there was more than one woman. Who got away?"

"You ask too many questions," said Pablo over the top of the magazine. He was obviously enjoying his new position of power.

"Was it Lassiter's woman? Was she the other one?"

"What fucking difference does it make?" Pablo sneered.

"None." George decided an appeal to the boy's ego might work. "I just thought you probably knew everything that was going on around here."

Pablo set the magazine aside. "Yeah, it was Señor Roy's woman."

As long as Pablo was willing to talk, George was willing to listen. "How'd they do it, Pablo?"

"They conked Julio on the head. Which is happening to you if you not shut the fuck up." Pablo picked up the magazine again and continued reading.

"No shit?" Rick interjected. "They cold cocked ol' Julio. What a pair of dames."

Julia hated violence, and George realized how desperate she must have been to be involved in such an act. Although he was concerned about his wife's safety, he couldn't help but smile inwardly at her audacity.

Haley stood up and leaned over the Judge's bed, looking out the window. "What do you make of this, George?"

"I don't know, sir." George didn't want to tell him in front of Pablo that Julia knew the way to get help. He wasn't even sure that she still had the compass.

Strand opened a bleary eye, finally roused by the commotion. "What's going on, Jack?"

"It seems that George's wife has escaped."

"What?" The Judge did his best to sit up in bed.

"Take it easy, Albert." Haley grasped the old man's shoulders and guided him gently back down. "Apparently Julia and the woman who was watching her have slipped off into the woods."

"Are they going to get help?" Strand said a little too loudly.

"We don't know." Haley leaned over the end of his bed and whispered to George, "What do you think their chances are?"

George looked up at his employers eyes. The anger was gone, replaced by doubt and fear, and perhaps a spark of hope. "I wish I knew," he said.

"Is there anything I should be aware of?" Haley asked.

George flicked his eyes toward Pablo, who was still poring over his magazine. Haley nodded knowingly and leaned back. George glanced across at Rick. "You okay?"

"Hey, this is a great camp." Rick shifted his weight, trying to get more comfortable. "Beds are a little hard, though."

"Yeah, well, tell your counselor." George closed his eyes and tried to imagine how Julia was doing, praying that she'd find safety before Brady's men found her.

Roy Lassiter had seldom felt more nervous. "I'm sorry, boss. We just can't seem to get a line on them two bitches." He studied Brady's face for any sign of reaction, but it was difficult to see much in the pine-filtered moonlight. Brady had stayed calm throughout the day's search. Judging by Roy's experience with his boss, that wasn't a good sign.

"Let me get this straight," Brady said. "Twelve men, searching for eighteen hours, haven't been able to find a single clue?"

"That's right. It's just like the woods swallowed 'em up. We can't even find a footprint."

Roy caught himself shifting nervously from foot to foot, and stopped himself. The guesthouse door banged shut as another jeep-load of men got ready to head back to the airstrip road. He'd sent Pablo to watch the hostages so Ramone could lend his more experienced eyes to the search.

Brady finally spoke. "Well, Roy, I guess you'll just have to try a little harder, won't you?"

Grateful for a break in the tension, Roy said, "Absolutely, boss. I've got every man up there now. Even Ramone."

"Who's watching our guests?"

"Pablo. He's a good man?"

Brady shook his head. "He's a boy. Ramone is more reliable."

"I needed Ramone to help out—he's from the country. When he was growing up, he spent a lot of time hunting. Pablo knows what he's doing."

"You'd better be right about that." Brady turned and went back into the cabin.

Roy had only seen Brady like this once before; the man responsible had ended up dead. Roy wasn't too optimistic about his own prospects, if he didn't find the women. He hurried down the porch steps and over to his jeep. He was reaching for his handheld radio when a sudden movement in the moonlight startled him. "Who the hell is that?"

"Me, Roy. Steve."

Roy scowled. "Where the fuck you been, Raimus?"

"Down by the lake, just drinking in the ambiance."

"You'll be sleeping in the lake if you don't help us find them two broads."

"Thanks for the advice, Roy. I'll take it up with Brady. You seen him?"

Roy grabbed the radio and turned it on. "He's in the cabin. Good luck, if you're going see him."

"He's not pissed at me. I'm not the one who fucked up."

"Yeah, well, good for you. Let me know how it went, dipshit."

Roy pressed his transmitter button. "Tony, where the hell are you?" Words came back, filtered by static: something about being lost. Roy swore.

Steve snorted. "I'd say you're the one who needs the luck." Then he went around the side of the cabin, toward the kitchen doorway.

Chapter 25

Julia could barely make Naomi out in the gathering gloom. The sun had set and the full moon was just rising over the ridge to the east. The day had almost been more than she could bear. They had hidden themselves in a dense thicket, but it had gotten awfully cold in the early hours, and they weren't dressed warmly enough. She'd huddled with Naomi for warmth, doing her best to get some sleep.

Voices had woken them early. Two of the searchers were nearby. Julia had seen a pair of alligator shoes through the underbrush—they were that close. But the men had kept going and were soon out of earshot. Julia toyed with the idea of working their way back to the compound during the day, but they both decided it would be too risky. With so many hunters, night was the women's friend.

Waiting for dark was no easy task either. The thicket was damp, and insects were a constant annoyance. Julia was nervous about what they had to do, but she was still glad when the evening grew dark enough for them to move.

"Lets get started," she said.

"We can't go back on that road."

"I know. We'll stay as deep in the woods as we can."

Naomi's dismay showed on her face.

"We can do it," Julia said. "We'll need the compass to help us stay on course, though."

Naomi opened the instrument and squinted at the luminous dial. She looked north. "Yeah, I guess we go off that way."

Julia pointed down the ridge. "We'll head a little way to the west before turning north, to make sure we stay deep in the woods. If we stay on track, we'll be there in an hour, maybe less. Do you think Roy and his boys will keep on searching that long?"

Naomi shrugged. "Who knows? Once Roy gets something in his head, it's pretty hard to get it knocked loose. One thing's for sure: they ain't gonna be looking for us near the cabins."

"You sure you want to go through with this? You could just slip off into the woods and head for civilization."

"Don't worry about me," Naomi said. "If I didn't want to do this, I damn well wouldn't. So let's get going." She set off along the ridge to the west.

Julia looked back towards the airstrip. She couldn't make anything out through the brush and darkness. She glanced up at the moon to get a fix on its location, then set off after Naomi.

Navigating the dense forest by moonlight was difficult, and their pace was slow but steady. After a while, Julia grabbed Naomi's arm. "Hold on a minute." She glanced up at the moon. "Check our bearing again."

Naomi fumbled with the compass. "Can't see the dial so good. The green stuff's gone all faint." She snapped it shut. "Seems like we should be there by now, don't it?"

"Yeah. I hope we didn't go too far west before we turned north. But even if we missed the camp, we should at least run into the lake, don't you think?"

"Hey, you're the damn girl scout around here."

"Well, let's head a little more in that direction." Julia pointed northeast. "We're bound to run across it sooner or later."

"If we don't get whopped to death by these branches first," Naomi said.

The underbrush had gotten considerably thicker as they continued to the north, and Julia's own face was scraped and bleeding from several encounters with branches that Naomi had let go too quickly as she went ahead. Julia ignored the discomfort. "We'll be there soon. I know it."

The taste of sweat and blood trickled onto her lips. She wiped her face with her jacket sleeve. As she raised her head, she glimpsed a sparkle of light off to the right, through the trees. Naomi had started moving again and was now about ten feet in front of her. Julia almost called out, but caught herself in time. She hurried to catch up, and grabbed Naomi by the back of her coat.

Naomi whirled around. "What the hell?"

"Shhh," Julia said. "I see it."

"What?"

"The camp." She pointed in the direction of the light. "Over there."

"I'll be damned." Naomi said.

"Come on." Julia set off toward the light, pushing her way through the underbrush.

They moved more quickly now, counting on the rising wind in the treetops to mask the sounds they made. Soon, they stood between two large pines trying to steady their breathing. About twenty feet away, through the lighted guesthouse window, they could just make out Pablo sitting near the front door and thumbing through a magazine.

"Now what?" whispered Naomi.

"Let's just wait and watch for a few minutes. Do you think Roy and the other men are back from their search yet?"

"I don't think so. Pablo is young. They wouldn't put him on guard if there was anyone else here."

"Then we'd better do something before they get back. Got any ideas?"

"Oh, great," Naomi said. "You drag me for miles through the woods and you don't have a clue what to do when we get here."

"Just give me a minute."

Naomi handed her Juan's gun. "Here."

"What the hell am I suppose to do with this?" Julia held the weapon gingerly, as if it were hot to the touch.

Naomi retrieved the gun and cycled a round into the chamber. "Never mind. Just follow me."

Julia stayed rooted to the spot, as if hypnotized by the gun in the other woman's hand. Naomi turned and beckoned her, then worked her way around to the front, ducking as she passed each window. Julia pulled herself together and followed.

When they reached the front door, Naomi motioned for Julia to stand off to the side. Then she took a deep breath and knocked on the door.

A startled voice from inside asked, "*Que es?*"

"Naomi. Open up," she said with as much authority as she could muster.

"Who?"

"Naomi, you greaseball. Open up before I have Roy slap you upside the head."

"Señor Roy?"

"Yeah, Seenyor Roy's gonna make a taco stuffing out of you if you don't open this goddamn door."

Julia held her breath, listening to footsteps approaching the door. The curtain that covered a small window in the door was pulled aside and Pablo's face appeared, his warm breath fogging the glass. Naomi pushed her own face closer so he could get a good look.

"What are you doing here?" he asked.

"I've got the woman. I brought her back." Naomi grabbed Julia's arm and pulled her into view. Startled, Julia struggled against her grip.

"I thought you were with her," said Pablo.

"I was just going along to see what she was up to. Now open the door . You want to be a big hero don't you?"

He stepped back and pulled the door open, and Naomi pushed the gun into his face. Pablo backed into the cabin. She nodded to the Uzi that hung under his arm. "Drop that."

Pablo stood blinking, his hand slowly dropping toward the Uzi. Naomi put the barrel of her gun against his forehead. "Just slip that thing off your shoulder. Slowly. Before I blow your *cabasa* open."

Beads of sweat formed on the young man's forehead as he carefully reached up to the strap over his shoulder, pulled it off, and let the weapon clatter to the floor. Julia, who had followed Naomi in, stepped around her and kicked the gun away.

It skittered to a stop at George's feet. "Julia! What the—"

Naomi interrupted. "Close the door, Julia." Then to Pablo, who was now standing against his chair: "Sit down, slimeball."

"You are crazy, Señora. Why do you do this?"

"You just shut up."

A safety catch clicked, and Julia whirled to see Jack Haley pointing the discarded Uzi at both Pablo and Naomi. "Jack, what are you doing?"

"Trying to find out what the hell is going on."

"Naomi's helping us get out of here," Julia answered. "She's on our side."

Haley looked at Naomi suspiciously. "Are you sure?"

"I'm sure."

"Okay." Haley lowered the Uzi. "What now what do we do?"

"We fly," said George.

Chapter 26

George stood close to Julia, who was sitting in the chair that Pablo had occupied just a few minutes earlier, dabbing the scratches on her face with a wet towel.

"This sounds like fun," Rick said. "Do you suppose Brady will light some fires for us so we can see the runway?" He put the finishing touches to Pablo's gag—he'd found a roll of duct tape and had wound most of it around the unfortunate youth's head. Pablo was now stretched out on Haley's bed, with his wrists and ankles cuffed to the iron frame. He was writhing like a trapped animal.

"Flying is the only chance we've got," George said.

"Can't we just head out on foot?"

George flicked his eyes toward the Judge. "We wouldn't get far." He glanced down at Julia. He could hardly believe he was with her again—and safe, for the moment at least.

"Maybe help will come," she said. "We went to the plane, and I contacted an airbus and told him our position."

"Nice work, but it's a long shot," George said. "Even if he believed you, we can't afford to wait."

"He's right," said Haley. "We've got to chance it."

Naomi had take the other chair, across the table from Julia. "Whatever you do, you better make it quick," she said. "Roy and the others ain't gonna leave Pablo on his own for long." She kept tapping her foot, and glancing over at the young gunman.

George nodded. "Yeah, we need to get going. Rick, help me with the Judge."

Rick moved to comply. "How far is the air strip?"

"About half a mile along the road," Julia answered. She glanced at the Judge. "But we're not going to be breaking any speed records. It'll take twenty minutes, maybe more."

Naomi was still looking at Pablo. "Will he keep that long?"

George went over to check the prisoner. The cuffs were tight, shackling Pablo's limbs to the bedstead. George knew from personal experience that there was no slipping out of those manacles. He checked Pablo's gag. "He's not going anywhere. Come on, let's get the Judge on his feet. We've got to get going."

"What's going on, Jack?" said Strand as they helped him up.

"We're getting out of here, Albert," said Haley.

"How?"

"George is going to fly us out, but first we have to get to the plane. Do you think you can make it?"

"Sure. Just point me in the right direction." Strand took two faltering steps, then sagged backward. George and Rick caught him under the arms.

"Take it easy, sir," said George. "Let us help you."

Julia peered out of the little window and then opened the door. She stepped outside, head cocked as she listened. Then she signaled the others to follow. Naomi held the door open as George and Rick guided the Judge outside. Haley followed and then Naomi closed the door, cutting off Pablo's muffled curses.

The little group gathered around the south side of the guesthouse. George looked toward the lake and saw movement in the darkness: a figure was approaching. "Shhh," he whispered. "Someone's coming. Stay close to the wall."

Everybody shrank back into the shadows. Haley breathed into George's ear, "Where?"

George pointed to the front of the cabin, where two figures stood near a parked jeep. The men talked for a while, then one moved around to the back of the main house. A slice of yellow light poured out of the open door, illuminating the ground. The figure went inside. George heard some faint voices until the door closed, cutting out both sound and light.

They remained motionless, watching the second man who was still standing by the jeep. George felt his throat close up as the man started walking toward the guesthouse. He pressed himself closer to the wall; so did everyone else.

The man came straight at them, but then he veered toward the other side of the little cabin and into the woods behind. He was swearing, continuously but softly. It sounded like Roy Lassiter.

George waited until everything was quiet again. "All right. Let's move." The group set off. Before they'd gone thirty feet, George could hear that the Judge was having problems: he was wheezing and gasping for breath. This was no good. "Julia, you and Naomi go on ahead and watch for anybody coming this way," he whispered. "Mr. Haley, would you bring up the rear?"

"Yes, George," Haley said.

"The first few yards are the most dangerous," said Julia. "Until you get into the shadow of the trees."

"We'll be as quick as we can," replied George.

"Okay. Here we go," said Julia. She and Naomi hurried across the moonlit ground, finally disappearing underneath the canopy of trees over the road.

George waited for a few seconds more to see if the hunters had noticed. He and Rick positioned themselves either side of the Judge and half guiding, half carrying him, crossed the open space. As soon as they were in the shadows, Haley made his way across the open ground. He paused just inside the opening of trees and studied the house and grounds carefully before continuing.

The going was slow. The Judge was a heavy load for all his frailty, and George and Rick had to stop every few minutes to catch their breath. During one of these pauses, George heard footsteps approaching from up ahead.

"What is it?" Rick whispered.

George stood frozen, the blood pounding in his temples. Fear grabbed at his heart until he heard Julia's voice. "George! It's me!" she whispered.

"You scared the crap out of us!"

"Sorry. We've been waiting at the end of the road, and I got worried about how long you were taking. Where's Mr. Haley?"

"Right here." Haley came up along beside the little group. "What's wrong?"

"Julia was trying to give us a coronary," said Rick.

"Where's Naomi?" asked Haley, a hint of suspicion in his voice.

Julia pointed toward the airstrip. "She's hiding in the trees, over there."

"Any sign of the men?" asked George.

"No. They must still be in the woods, looking for us."

"They don't give up easy," said Rick.

George nodded. "They have a lot at stake."

They all turned to the sound of running footsteps. It was Naomi. "They're coming!" she said breathlessly when she reached the group.

She had just gotten the words out when a revving jeep engine sounded from the direction of the airstrip. "Damn!" said George. "Get the Judge off the road!"

George and Rick hustled Strand toward the underbrush. Haley helped from behind, but the bushes were dense and it was slow work. The jeep was getting louder. "Hurry up!" Naomi said in a hoarse whisper.

Headlights flashed through the trees a hundred yards away, scattering shadows in all directions. In seconds, they'd be caught in the beams.

Julia grabbed Naomi and charged into Haley, cannoning him into the other three men. Everybody went down. Before anyone could react, the jeep went speeding by.

They all lay quietly, until the silence was broken by a moan from the Judge. Haley was the first to extricate himself from the pile. "Albert! Are you all right?"

The old man just moaned again.

"Be careful, Mr. Haley. Your knee is in my back," said Rick.

"Shhh!" whispered George. "Somebody might be following on foot."

They waited.

"No one's coming, George," Haley said. "We've got to see if Albert is all right."

Julia and Naomi helped Rick and George get the Judge to his feet. Haley brushed the old man off. "Albert, are you okay?"

"That was a hell of a tumble." Strand's voice was barely audible, but at least he didn't seem to have taken any serious hurt.

They worked their way back up onto the road. This time, Julia and Naomi helped with the Judge. Haley brought up the rear again, listening for any sign of pursuit.

Steve Raimus found Brady pacing the kitchen floor. "Hey man, what's up? You don't look so good."

"Shut the door, Raimus. You're letting in the goddamn mosquitoes."

"Okay, no need to bite my head off." Steve closed the door.

Brady stared at him intently. "So, where the hell have you been?"

"I was talking to Roy. He said you're pissed about the women getting away."

"He did, eh? Well, he's right. If he doesn't find them soon he's going to be in a world of shit..."

Steve did his best not to smile at Roy's misfortune. So much for you, you arrogant bastard, he thought. Who's the dipshit now?

But Brady hadn't finished: "...and so are you, Raimus."

Steve flinched, and any thought of smiling vanished. "But I didn't have anything to do with them getting away."

"You should have warned me about his wife."

"Julia? You knew her as well as I did. Shit, I'd never met her before Chicago. How was I to know she was crazy?"

"You were right there as she went along with George's half-baked plan. No woman in her right mind would've let that happen, let alone insist on coming along."

"Ashton...what a pussy-whipped son-of-a-bitch he is."

Brady didn't respond to that. "If we don't find them soon, we're going to have to move the whole operation. That wouldn't make me happy."

Steve stared at the floor.

"Do me a favor, Raimus. Go over to the guesthouse and check on Pablo."

"Pablo? What do you want me to do?"

"I don't know. Just make sure he doesn't fuck up."

"Why doesn't Roy go?"

"Because I'm telling you to! Jesus, Raimus, make yourself useful for a change."

"Whatever." Steve did his best to look nonchalant, but he still couldn't bring himself to look at Brady as he went to the door.

Chapter 27

Steve stood outside for a moment, trying to let the fresh air and cool night soothe his nerves, and giving his eyes time to readjust to the darkness. The moon was almost directly ahead and it didn't take long. He strolled towards the smaller cabin, enjoying the cheery glow of its windows.

He listened for a moment at the front door, but heard nothing. Maybe everyone was asleep...but then why were the lights on? He didn't want to disturb them. A light tap at the door, perhaps, just to see if Pablo was awake...

His knock was answered with a banging from inside the cabin. He rapped a little louder. The banging seemed to increase.

"Pablo, you in there?" He tried the handle. The door opened and he stepped inside. There was Pablo, handcuffed and gagged, writhing insanely on the bed.

"Holy shit! Pablo, what happened?"

Pablo made an urgent, muffled groan. Steve pulled the gag from his mouth, releasing a rapid string of Spanish.

"Pablo, Pablo. Calm down and speak English. What happened?"

Eventually, the Spanish became interspersed with enough English for Steve to piece it together.

"Whores! Crazy whores! Take men! Dead fucking loco whores! Dead fucking everybody!"

"Where'd they go?" Steve asked.

Pablo broke into another stream of Spanish.

This was not good. If Brady was pissed about the two women, losing the main prizes was going to send him ballistic. Steve swore. What was he supposed to do? "All right, all right, Pablo. Calm down." He paced around the room, searching for some sign that would indicate where they might have gone.

Pablo jangled his handcuffs against the bedstead. "Get these fucking things off me!"

"Where's the key?"

"I don't know. Just get them off!"

Pablo cursed and rattled the manacles while Steve hunted for the keys. It was useless. "They must've taken them," Steve said. "Maybe there's some boltcutters, or we could dismantle the bed…Fuck! Brady is not going to be happy about this."

Pablo stopped struggling. "No, no, please don't tell Señor Keyes!"

Steve wasn't crazy about the idea himself, but what else could he do? "Pablo, how in the hell do you think he's not going to find out about this?"

"Just get me out of these, Señor, I will find them, pronto."

"If you think I want Brady finding out that I didn't tell him about this, you're out of your mind."

"Señor, please. Señor Keyes will kill me."

Steve couldn't blame Pablo for being desperate. Brady might well kill the kid and that would be too bad, but Steve wasn't about to put his neck in the noose too. "Señor Keyes is a reasonable man. I'm sure he'll give you the opportunity to make things right. I'm going to get help. Just relax and don't worry."

Outside, it was strangely quiet. There had been a breeze before, but it had dissipated. Steve decided to take a moment to steady his nerves: there'd be time enough for confrontation later, so why not enjoy the peace while he could? He was in no hurry to face Keyes with news of this latest disaster.

As he waited, several dark figures emerged from the woods behind the main house. "Some of the boys back from beating the bushes?" he wondered. But these didn't appear to be any of Brady's or Roy's men, who were constantly jabbering to each other about ruining their Italian loafers or silk shirts in the brush. These were like ghosts.

Why were they moving so stealthily, this close to the cabins?

Steve took a step forward. "What the hell?"

Before he could utter another word, a strong hand had came out of nowhere and clamped itself over his mouth. Something dug painfully into his back, and a sharp edge pressed against his throat. Steve swiveled his eyes down and saw the glint of steel.

"Be still," a menacing voice whispered into his ear from behind. "Don't do anything stupid. Nod if you understand."

In spite of the strong grip, Steve managed to move his head slightly up and down. He heard a brief commotion from inside the guesthouse behind him, muffled by the door.

"Drop to the ground. Keep it slow. Face down."

With the knife still at his throat, Steve complied. Once on the ground, the pain in his back, created by the man's knee, seemed to intensify, but he didn't speak.

"Now, when I remove my hand from your mouth you won't make a sound, right partner?" said the voice.

Steve did his best to nod. Slowly the hand slipped away from his face and down along his side to his right wrist. It bent his right arm behind his back. At last the pressure on his back eased and the knife disappeared from his throat. The downside was that both arms were now behind his back and plastic handcuffs were being applied.

"Very good, partner."

Steve tried to ask what was happening, but before he could get the words out, a large slab of tape was stuck over his mouth.

"What's that, partner?"

Steve mumbled again.

"That's what I thought you said." The man rose and moved toward the door of the guesthouse. He eased it open. "Everything okay in there?"

A voice from the cabin whispered back. "Yeah. We're clear."

"Is the Judge okay?"

There was a brief silence, then the other voice whispered. "He's not here."

The man stepped inside.

Steve struggled to rise, but fell backward against the outside wall of the structure. At least he was on his side now, which meant he could see something. Lights were moving around the perimeter of the compound; more lights blazed from the main house. Steve managed to roll into a sitting position, and then to his knees. Slowly, he straightened until his head was level with the sill of the window above him. He could make out individual voices.

"...if I knew where they are, I no tell you assholes," Pablo said.

"Listen, partner, you tell me or I'll throw you and this bed frame in that lake out there, you hear me?"

The other voice was talking into a radio, repeating the same message: "...Red Dog Three to Red Dog leader, we've secured the guesthouse but subjects are not present. I repeat, subjects not present. Red Dog Three to Red Dog leader..."

Steve scuffed the tape gag against his shoulder until he'd loosened a corner, and then chewed and shook his head until he got rid of the thing. A shame the cuffs wouldn't be so easy, he thought... He slipped around the south side of the cabin, then stumbled across the opening to the road leading to the airstrip and disappeared beneath the arch of trees. But instead of following the road into the woods, he hid behind the large propane pig located a few feet off the road to his right. He needed to get his bearings and figure out who these people were and where they were coming from.

The unmistakable *whump whump whump* of a helicopter cut through the night. A dark shape passed almost directly overhead, just above the treetops, and hovered above the south end of the yard, behind the main house. A second helicopter approached across the lake. Within seconds, lights on the two choppers illuminated the entire compound. Steve wished he could shield his eyes from the brightness. All he could do was to burrow into the shadow of the metal tank.

A loud yell pulled his attention to the front of the guesthouse. The man who'd handcuffed him was standing on the spot where he'd left Steve. He switched on a flashlight and played it around the area. Steve huddled lower behind the tank as the beam, competing with the chopper searchlights, flashed above his head. The man started to move toward him.

Steve was frozen by fear. Everything was happening too fast.

The light moved away. Steve edged up toward the top of the tank so he could peer across the opening between him and the guesthouse. The man was still there, his light dangling from the hand at his side. He was speaking into a throat microphone.

Steve tried to make out what he was saying, but it was too quiet and the helicopters were too loud. The chopper hovering over the main house moved forward and descended slowly, preparing to land in the backyard. The other chopper swung back around and took off to the west, its light just passing to the right of the propane tank, then dancing off branches behind him.

A length of angled steel jutted from the foundation of the propane tank. Steve pushed the handcuffs over it, and twisted. It hurt like hell, but the plastic gave a little. So did his skin: he could feel blood trickling over his fingers. He stifled a hysterical laugh and twisted again. The plastic gave some more, and this time he managed to slip free.

The man who'd captured him was still nearby, and now Steve could hear what he was saying: "Roger that," and then out loud to his partner, "Mike, let's go. Dog Two has a pack of rats holed up in the woods, and needs some help."

By the time the one called Mike hurried out of the guesthouse, his partner was already crashing through the woods behind the little cabin. Mike followed. Steve listened until the sounds of their passing had faded. He was about to move when a burst of gunfire sounded from the trees in the direction where the two men were headed.

His knees were shaking so violently, he almost couldn't stand. He steadied himself against the metal tank, watching as the rotors of the helicopter behind the main house wound down.

Who were these guys? Obviously some kind of a SWAT team, but whose, and how did they get here? How long had the camp been under surveillance?

More importantly, how the hell was he going to get out?

Several minutes passed, men scurrying here and there around the house and gunfire still echoing in the woods behind him. The rear door of the main house opened again and two figures emerged. They were both dressed in SWAT-type clothing, but one moved with a gait that seemed strangely familiar. Steve strained to see. As the figures passed by the light of the kitchen window, Steve got a good look at the man's face, and blanched. "Son of a bitch!" he said under his breath. "Santez has given him an out!"

The engine whined and the rotors began to turn. Steve watched as Brady and the other man approached the aircraft. Just before he hopped in to the chopper, Brady clapped his SWAT team companion on the shoulder and smiled. The rotors picked up speed, the ship straining to leave the ground. Steve became aware of a disturbance behind him. Someone was approaching through the woods. Steve scrambled toward the end of the tank—he didn't want to move around the front of it, because of the helicopter, but he didn't want his back exposed either.

The helicopter rose and swung around toward the south as Roy emerged from the woods between the guesthouse and the propane tank. He paused, breathing hard and blinking at what he saw. His clothes were dirty and torn; Steve could make out a dark stain over his right breast. His right arm hung limply, but his left hand clutched an Uzi which now rose, tracking the path of the helicopter.

The muzzle flash split the night. Steve had to look away, toward the helicopter. Pinpoint sparks appeared as Roy's bullets struck the ship. The chopper swung like an angry bird of prey, seeking the source of it's torment. The dark predatory shape lit up with return flashes, and dirt flew as the bullets felt their way toward Roy.

Then the helicopter began to oscillate, at first gently and then more wildly. Smoke billowed out, shrouding the muzzle flashes, but the bird's return fire was still visible—except that bullets were now spraying the entire area.

Steve backed away from the propane tank, hating to abandon its shelter but driven by its deadly potential. A burst of automatic fire slammed into Roy and tossed him, broken, to the ground. Overhead, the helicopter was in trouble too: out of control and on its way down. Steve ran for his life, but something compelled him to turn his head for one last look at the tank.

The explosion was the last thing he ever saw.

Chapter 28

Once they reached *Haley's Comet,* George directed Julia, Haley and Naomi to take down the camouflage netting. Then he opened the fuselage door and felt his way up the steps. He turned to help Rick hoist Judge Strand up.

They almost had the Judge inside when George heard something, and froze.

"Come on, George, I can't do this on my own," said Rick.

"Hush!"

Everybody stopped what they were doing and looked at George, who was staring at the sky. "Hear that?"

A low-flying helicopter was approaching from the south. Within seconds, it passed overhead, flying without running lights and barely visible against the night sky.

"What do you make of that?" Haley asked.

"Maybe Julia's radio message got through." George turned back to his task. "But we're still not going to wait around."

Once the Judge was settled, George sent Rick to help with the netting. Then he went to the flight deck to prepare the airplane for start-up. A few minutes later, Rick stuck his head inside. "All set out here."

George hurried back past the Judge and down the steps to help turn the aircraft around. Before they'd completed the task, gunfire erupted in the distance.

"Some bad shit's going on back there," Rick said.

"None of our business," George replied. "We need to get

this plane in the air." They continued turning the plane. Before they'd finished, a huge explosion rocked the night and a fireball lit up the sky to the north.

Everybody stood frozen as a second, smaller explosion echoed the first. Then all was quiet.

"Help me!" George snapped, pushing against the fuselage. The other men threw themselves into the task, turning *Haley's Comet* through 180 degrees in the soft grass.

They had gathered at the plane's door when a voice called out behind them. "It seems I'm just in time. A few minutes later and I'd have missed my flight."

Brady Keyes stepped out of the shadows. He was dressed in some kind of ripped uniform, and looked like he'd been through hell. He moved stiffly, but that took nothing from the air of nonchalance with which he pointed his 9mm. "What? Not glad to see me?"

George could barely speak. "How—?"

"Did you really think you'd get away with fucking me over, Little Wing? Carlos has tentacles everywhere, even in the RCMP."

"The what?" Rick asked.

"The Mounties, to you. A young officer can boost his paycheck quite handsomely, just for ignoring the occasional unauthorized shipment from South America."

"You people disgust me," George said.

"Oh, don't get all high and mighty. Just because you wear a uniform doesn't mean you're a Boy Scout. Would you rather be trolling for women in a BMW, or a Yugo?"

George took a closer look at Brady's clothing: SWAT gear, though ripped and bloodied. "What happened to you, Brady?"

"Let's just say my ride was involved in a little accident. But now I have new one." Brady waved the gun in the direction of *Haley's Comet.*

"Where's, Roy?" Naomi asked.

"I have no idea, and I care even less."

"If you're going to kill us, get it over with," Haley said. "Otherwise, get the hell out of our way."

"Oh, I'm not going to kill you." He nodded at George. "Your boy here fucked everything up, and now he's going to get me out of this. By the way, where is the honorable Judge Strand?"

"He's inside," said George. "He needs a doctor."

"He's going to need an undertaker if you don't cooperate. Now let's get this thing ready to go."

George nodded to the others. "Just do as he says." He moved to the airplane, to examine it.

Brady said, "No time for that preflight shit. Just get it started and let's go." He herded the little group up the steps and into the airplane. "George, get up front and turn on some lights in here." Julia made to follow, but Brady grabbed her by the arm. "I want you right here. Naomi, you go with him." He slammed Julia into the nearest seat and sat down opposite her, his gun pointing at her chest and looked around at the others. "The first slip, and this bitch gets a hole in her heart. Then I'll be looking for someone to replace her."

George had to tear himself away. To stay would have been to put Julia in more danger. He led the way to the cockpit, slipped into the left seat, and flicked the cabin lights on. Naomi stood behind him. He indicated the right seat. "Sit here."

He busied himself with the task of restarting the engines and preparing for takeoff. "Where are we going?" he yelled back to Brady.

"Just level off above the trees. I'll tell you where we're going when we are airborne. And leave the goddamn transponder off."

While the engines were spooling up, George yelled back, "Make sure everyone is buckled up; this is going to be rough." He stood on the brakes and pushed the throttles forward. At peak RPM, he released the brakes. *Haley's Comet* leapt forward, bouncing along the uneven ground. Naomi braced herself against the top of the instrument panel.

"Don't worry, we'll make it." George wished he really believed it.

Racing past the halfway point of the runway, George saw that the plane hadn't built up enough speed to rotate. It had to be the extra weight of the passengers—too late to do anything about it now. He added 10 more degrees of flap and, as though trying to squeeze out extra power, pushed harder on the throttles.

The trees at the end of the runway were looming large. Naomi yelled, "We're not going to make it!"

George ignored her, concentrating on the airspeed indicator. The instant the needle crossed 97 knots, he pulled back on the yoke. The nose drifted skyward, the plane still shaking and bucking as if it would tear itself apart. Then the bouncing stopped as the wheels left the ground. Trees filled the windshield, and George jammed the landing gear lever to the up position. He continued to pull the nose up until the plane reached the speed allowing the greatest angle of climb. Holding his breath, he swore that he heard branches scraping the fuselage as the tree tops flashed below.

Chapter 29

George's breath whistled between his teeth as *Haley's Comet* leveled off a mere hundred feet above the trees.

"Jesus," Naomi said. "I thought you was trying to take us all out!"

Ignoring the remark, George called back to the passenger compartment. "Is everyone all right?"

"We're okay, but I think we'll have to break out the airsick bags," Rick shouted back.

"I told you it was going to be rough. So Brady, where the hell are we going?"

"Hibbing, Minnesota."

"That's gotta be well over 300 miles and we have less than an hour of fuel. We'll be on fumes."

"We'll make it. I'm not exactly worried about FAA regulations at the moment. Just dial it in on your GPS and don't try to fuck with me, Little Wing."

George pulled out a sectional map from the pocket next to his seat, handed it to Naomi, and turned on the light above her seat.

"What the hell am I supposed to do with this?" she said.

"Open it up and find Hibbing, Minnesota for me."

"Hibbing what?"

"Hibbing, Minnesota. I need the airport designation for the GPS."

"I never heard of no Hibbing, Minnesota."

"It's there. Just look for me, okay?"

She opened the map and stared at the myriad of lines and symbols on the aeronautical chart. "I can't make heads or tails out of this shit."

"Then grab the wheel and hand me that."

"Grab what?"

"The wheel." George reached over and put Naomi's hand on the control wheel. "Just hold this steady and keep us from crashing into the trees."

"You're crazy! I'll kill us!"

"No you won't, Naomi. Just hold it steady for a few seconds while I look at the map. We're too low for me to do both."

George held the wheel with her for a while until he was reasonably sure that Naomi had the feel. Then he let go. Immediately the nose rose skyward. George grabbed the wheel again and leveled it off. "Just relax and keep it from moving one way or the other."

He let go again and quickly searched the map for Hibbing's designation. There it was...HIB. He grabbed the wheel again. "Okay, Naomi. Good job."

Naomi looked over at him. "You must have some kind of a death wish, man."

George glanced down at the GPS. "Turn that dial." He pointed to the unit, and Naomi complied. An 'H' appeared in the display. "That's it." He had her repeat the process until 'I' and 'B' were also dialed in. The GPS provided the course, and he gently banked the plane around to match the recommended heading. Then he settled into flying the plane, concentrating on the task of cruising at treetop level with only 100 feet to absorb any mistake.

<hr>

The morning sun was blazing into the cockpit as they approached Hibbing. George was close to the end of his resources, but fear and anger helped counter his fatigue. As soon as he could see the airport, he called back to Brady, "We're almost there. Now what?"

"Land this thing. What the hell else?"

"I'll have to gain some altitude to set up for a proper landing."

Brady didn't respond, so George configured the airplane for a slow climb. They passed over the mid-section of runway 13 from the northeast to the southwest at two thousand feet. Nothing appeared to be moving at the small airport, but there on the tarmac in front of the fuel pumps was a Gulfstream II, looking out of place among the Cessnas and Pipers.

Turning to the downwind leg, he went through the pre-landing checklist, made sure everyone in the rear was set, lowered the gear and set the flaps. Turning to final, he crabbed slightly to the left compensate for the mild crosswind component and kicked a little right rudder to line the nose with the runway centerline. The mains greased on the pavement and the nosegear soon followed to complete the perfect landing.

As the airplane rolled out to the end of the runway, George yelled to Brady, "Now what?"

"Taxi over to that Gulfstream."

George turned on to the taxiway that led to the fuel pumps, and *Haley's Comet* rocked gently to a stop along side the Gulfstream. The whole airport seemed deserted. The jet looked empty, too. He unfastened his seat belts and went into the passenger compartment. Brady was gazing out the window at the Gulfstream. He was holding his shoulder, and when he looked up at George, he winced slightly. "You're doing fine so far, Little Wing. Don't try to be a hero and screw it up now." He leaned forward and pointed his gun at Julia's head.

"We've done what you asked," George said.

"Not quite everything," Brady replied. "Something doesn't look quite right with my ride. I'm going to need the help of all you good folks just a little longer."

"What's that supposed to mean?"

"For starters, I'm going to need you to locate the pilot to that thing." Brady nodded toward the Gulfstream.

"How?"

"Go outside and find out what is going on. Start by checking out that airplane."

George glanced at each of his companions. Naomi was still up in the cockpit, but she'd twisted around to see into the passenger compartment. She looked defiant, but George knew she was scared. Haley was tending to the Judge, who kept drifting in and out of consciousness. Rick just looked back at him like he was waiting for orders. Lastly, George turned to Julia. She smiled weakly, but she couldn't hide her fear.

"Go find out what's happening, and report back to me, and she'll be alright," Brady said. "Just make sure nothing goes wrong, because if it does I won't hesitate to blow her head off." He glanced around. "And then the others. Understand?"

George nodded and met Julia's eyes again. "I'll be back."

He went to the door, opened it and lowered the steps. Outside, he found himself squinting in the bright sunshine. He made his way around the tail section of *Haley's Comet*. Why was the airport so quiet, on a day that would have every general aviation pilot itching to get airborne? As he rounded the plane, he looked up and saw Brady staring at him through the window.

Then he turned away and crossed the twenty yards of hot pavement between the two airplanes. The door to the passenger compartment was on the opposite side of the Gulfstream, so he circled around the sleek jet. The door was open; he climbed the steps and leaned inside. There was no sign of activity. "Anyone here?"

There was no answer, so he entered and began to move down the aisle. This was obviously a new airplane.

"Hold it right there," said a man's voice from the cockpit behind him.

George froze. A heavy-set man stepped out of the bathroom at the rear of the airplane, brandishing a machine pistol. "Raise your hands slowly and clasp your fingers behind your head."

George complied, and the man from the cockpit grabbed his right wrist and cuffed it. In one smooth move, he pulled George's right arm down behind his back and secured it to his left wrist. Then he spun George around and pushed him into a plush leather seat. The second man grabbed George from behind, forcing his shoulders back against the seat.

Dazed, George stared up at the captor who had just handcuffed and manhandled him into the seat. The man was tall, wearing a crumpled dark suit. A curly cable ran from his ear down to his collar. He stooped, bringing his face close to George's. "Where is Judge Strand?"

George breathed a sigh of relief: these were obviously not Carlos Santez's men. "I'm George Ashton."

"I don't care if you're the fucking Pope. Where is Judge Strand?"

"Do you mind if I ask who you are?"

The tall man pulled open his jacket to reveal an FBI badge hanging on his belt. "FBI Agent Carr. This is Agent Howard. Now, where's the Judge?"

George nodded in the direction of *Haley's Comet.* "He's in the King Air."

"Is he alive?"

"Yes, but he needs a doctor."

"Is Haley with him?"

"Yes. Look, I'm on your side. I've been—"

Carr interrupted. "Who did you say you are?"

"George Ashton. I'm the pilot."

"You work for Brady Keyes, right?" Howard asked, from behind.

"No, I don't work for Brady Keyes. I was blackmailed. He kidnapped my wife. I've got to get back to that plane."

"Blackmailed?"

"Keyes threatened to kill her if I didn't help him capture the Judge."

"You mean there are other hostages?" Carr glanced at his colleague and raised an eyebrow.

"Yes," George said. "There are four others."

"Including Haley and Strand?"

"No, in addition to them."

"Who?"

"My wife, Julia Ashton, Rick Vanbrough, and Naomi. I don't know her last name."

"That's only three," said Howard.

"I'm the fourth. Look, I've got to get back." George tried to struggle to his feet.

Carr pushed him back down. "Just hold on, fella."

"There's no time. I'll tell you everything later, but I've got to get back to the plane. He's going to kill Julia."

Carr looked at the other man. "Keep an eye on him. I'll contact Luscomb."

Howard came around and sat on the arm of the seat across from George. "Just relax."

George couldn't make out what Carr was saying as he walked away, but he seemed to be mumbling into a small microphone attached to the inside pocket of his jacket. George craned his head to see around Howard, and looked in the direction of *Haley's Comet*, but the Jet sat a little higher than the King Air. All he could see was the top of the other airplane.

"Trying to signal your buddies?" Howard asked.

"I'm trying to see if my wife is okay. If Keyes thinks anything's wrong, he's going to kill her."

"She'll be alright if you're telling the truth." Howard paused. "What's her name?"

"I told you—Julia Ashton."

"And you claim that she's not part of this?"

"No, and neither am I." Howard looked skeptical, so George plunged on: "At least, not really. Brady Keyes kidnapped Julia to force me to hijack—"

Before he could finish, Carr returned. "Luscomb wants to talk to this guy." He unhooked a two-way radio from his belt and handed it to George. "Just press the key on the side."

George shrugged his shoulders to remind Carr that he was handcuffed. "Oh yeah," said Carr. He tossed the radio into George's lap and took a couple of steps back up the aisle, pulled out his gun and trained it on George. "Uncuff him."

George leaned forward so Howard could remove the handcuffs. Once free, he massaged his wrists for a moment, then picked up the radio.

Carr nodded. "Just press the key on the side and speak into it."

George pressed the key. "George Ashton with you."

He released the transmit key and the radio crackled. "Ashton, I'm Agent Luscomb. We've commandeered this airport and have you and your plane under surveillance. There is no way out. Do you understand?"

"Yes, but—"

"You claim you are not working for Keyes. Is that right?"

"Yes. Keyes kidnapped my wife to blackmail me into helping him."

"Can you verify that?"

"Not right now. You've got to believe me. Julia's in that plane and Brady's got a gun to her head. I've got to get back to her."

"I understand that Haley and Strand are on the plane. Who else?"

"I already told these guys: Rick Vanbrough and Naomi, I don't know her last name."

"That would be Naomi Worthington. She's a known associate of Roy Lassiter," Luscomb said.

"She is, but she's been helping us."

"Why would she do that?"

"All I know is that she's in as much danger as the rest of us. Tell your men that she's a hostage, too."

"We'll keep it in mind," said Luscomb.

"What's your plan now? Brady is—"

Luscomb cut across him. "We're still assessing the situation. Put Agent Carr back on."

George handed over the radio. Carr walked back up the aisle, murmuring into the transmitter. Then he returned. "Luscomb wants to speak to you again." He handed over the radio.

George keyed the microphone. "Ashton here."

"George, I asked Agent Carr if he thought we could trust you."

"What'd he say?"

"He believes so. Is he right?"

"Of course he's right. I've been telling you all along that I'm not working for Keyes."

"I hope he is, because we need your help."

"My help? What are you going to do?"

"We're going bring this thing to an end."

George became agitated. "You're not going to storm the plane, are you? Not with Julia and Naomi still in there?"

"Our first priority is to secure the safety of the hostages."

"How?" asked George.

"We'd prefer to negotiate. At least initially."

"Assuming he'll talk to you, what will you offer him?"

"Safe passage out of here, in exchange for releasing the hostages unharmed," said Luscomb.

"How will you establish communications with Keyes?"

"That's where you come in. Will you help us?"

"Of course," George said, "but we've got to move. Brady is probably getting suspicious already."

Chapter 30

George made his way back around *Haley's Comet*. He didn't think much of Luscomb's plan, but he couldn't come up with anything better. There was no telling what Brady would do when he told him what was going on. George prayed that Brady's sense of self-preservation would overcome his anger.

He paused at the base of the stairs and took a deep breath before launching himself upward. Brady swung the gun around so it pointed directly at George as he entered the doorway. With his free hand, he grabbed Julia by the arm. She winced but didn't utter a sound. George fought back an urge to rush Brady.

"Where the hell have you been?" Brady asked.

"Doing what you told me to do. Checking out the airplane," said George.

"I didn't think it would take all day. Where's the crew?"

"They're not there."

"Well, where the fuck are they?"

"They're in custody."

Brady leaned forward. Julia shrank away from him, but he dragged her back. "Little Wing, I'm not in a mood for kidding."

"It's over, Brady. The place is crawling with FBI."

Keyes loosened his grip on Julia and leaned back. He didn't say anything; his face was a mask. Then he reclined even further and crossed his legs. He spread his arms across the seat backs, the gun pointing no where in particular.

"Well, well, Little Wing. You seem to have made some new friends," he said.

"They were waiting in the jet. As soon as I walked in, they jumped me."

"And then they let you go. Why would they do that?"

"Because they want to talk to you, and thought I'd make a better messenger than they would."

"You've got balls," Brady said with a tight smile.

"You're holding the aces."

Brady leaned forward again and took Julia's arm again. His eyes flashed. "Good of you to remember that." he said. "So, what do these fuckers want?"

"They want to talk to you." George produced the radio Carr had given him. Brady pulled Julia closer.

"Take it easy, Brady, it's just a radio." George handed it over.

Brady studied the radio for few seconds. Then he glanced around the plane at the others. Everyone stared back at him. He let go of Julia's arm and swung the gun around toward George.

"Just press the mike key," George said.

"I know how to work a goddamn radio." Brady pressed the key. "Yeah?"

"Is this Keyes?"

"Yeah. So, what the hell do you want?"

"Keyes, this is Agent Luscomb. I've got a proposition for you."

"I'll bet you do."

"Let Strand, Haley and the others go and you and your Colombian crew can take the Gulfstream back to Santez."

"You must think I'm pretty stupid, Luscomb."

"This is no joke, Keyes. We're willing to trade for the hostages."

"Yeah, I understand. You get what you want and I get dead."

"We have no intention of interfering with your escape. Just let the hostages leave the plane."

"Why would I want to give up my only ticket out of here?"

"You're going to have to give them up sooner or later. Why not now?"

"If I can make it to Colombia, I'm home free. Half the military is on Santez's payroll."

"Not as many as he's led you to think, Keyes. We have more influence than you imagine."

"You're full of shit, Luscomb."

"Your only way out of this is to cooperate."

Keyes put down the radio and glared at George. "You know Little Wing, this is precisely why I wanted to fuck with the government of this country in the first place. They're so stupid, they're practically begging for it."

"Brady, this is really your only way out," George said.

"Let me get this straight: I give up all my cards, and Luscomb and the rest of his little G-men give me my pilots and that jet over there, and let me fly back to Colombia. Is that right?"

"He gave me his word, Brady."

"You always were so goddamn gullible, Little Wing."

Luscomb's voice crackled over the radio. "Keyes, you there?" Brady ignored it.

"How far do you think you'd get with every Air Force in the Western Hemisphere tracking you?" George asked.

"A lot further than if I let Strand and the rest of you go."

Brady picked up the radio. "I have a counterproposal. I'll give you Haley but not the Judge. You give me a pilot and let us gas up the King Air and leave. Nobody follows us. We'll proceed to another airport, where we're allowed to refuel. I'll drop off one more. We'll follow that routine until I'm safely back in Colombia, where I'll turn the Judge over to your embassy."

The radio remained silent. Brady asked, "You hear me, Luscomb?"

"I hear you. We'll get back to you."

Chapter 31

Inside the tiny airport office, Agent Roberto Hernandez donned the leather flying jacket that had belonged to the Gulfstream pilot. It was little on the tight side, but close enough. In fact, it looked pretty fine. That wasn't much consolation for the task he had to do. He waited as Agents Neubacher and Fredericks pulled on their T-shirts, donated by the airport manager.

Luscomb was going through the briefing again: "This is all about timing, men. Neubacher, you have to get Keyes's attention while you're fueling the plane, but don't get too cute. Hernandez, when you think the time is right, make your move. We just need a few seconds. Carr and Howard will be outside the door, ready to assist you right away. Neubacher and Fredericks will be on their way too."

"You sure you don't want me to go out there with them?" the airport manager asked.

"Thanks, but we can handle it," said Neubacher.

The manager grumbled, "I should be out there. Refueling that King Air ain't as easy as it sounds. Just describing it ain't enough."

"We appreciate your offer, but we've got it covered. There are already too many civilians at risk," said Luscomb.

"Ready when you are, Robbie," Neubacher said.

"I'm ready," Hernandez answered.

Luscomb looked at him. "You sure you want to do this?"

"Sure, boss. No problem."

"Don't underestimate Keyes. He's a dangerous hombre."

"Don't worry, boss. I can handle it. Besides, I'll have plenty of backup."

"Okay, men. Move out."

***

George watched two men approach *Haley's Comet* across the tarmac. "Must be the line crew coming to fuel the plane."

Brady looked over his shoulder. "That one's a little old to be a pump jockey."

George thought it looked strange too, but he wasn't about to agree. "Could be the FBO manager. Probably doesn't want to endanger one of the kids." He couldn't tell if Brady was buying it. "Here comes the pilot."

"Never saw that guy before. Let him in, Little Wing."

By the time George got to the door and swung it open, the pilot was at the bottom of the steps. George stepped back. As the pilot passed, he gave George a funny look. Something had to be going on.

Brady seemed to think so, too. He pointed his gun at the young pilot, and asked him something in Spanish.

"Juan Navarro," the pilot answered.

"I don't remember you," Brady said.

"I just started working for Senior Santez a few weeks ago."

"Why would Carlos Santez send a brand new pilot on trip like this?" Brady asked.

Hernandez shrugged. "How would I know?"

Brady waved his gun toward the cockpit. "You know how to fly one of these?"

"Yes."

A loud bang sounded outside the plane.

"What the fuck?" Brady turned in the direction of the sound, looking out the window. George looked too. One of the fuelers had slammed a ladder against the wing. The other was yelling at him.

Brady snorted. "What a couple of idiots—"

The pilot jumped him. He chopped Brady across the neck. Brady dropped his gun and staggered back. The pilot—or agent, as George now understood him to be—wrestled his opponent to the floor. With one knee on Brady's back, he pulled his own gun from beneath his jacket and pressed it to the back of Brady's head.

Two more figures entered the plane: Howard and Carr, George realized. "Right behind you, Hernandez," Carr shouted to the fake pilot.

It had happened so fast that George was stunned. Julia lay sprawled on the floor where she'd been pushed in Hernandez's initial attack. George moved to help her. As he stooped over her, Howard jostled him and knocked him to the floor on top of her. "You okay?" he asked, his face an inch away from hers.

"I'm okay."

"Nice play, Robbie," said Carr.

"Thanks," Hernandez replied. "How about giving me a hand here?"

Brady began thrashing around. "Get off me!" Howard and Carr piled in to help Hernandez immobilize him.

One of the fuelers leaned through the door. "You guys all right?"

"Yeah, we've got Keyes under control," Carr said over Brady's stream of obscenities. "Get the rest of these people out of here."

The fueler beckoned to George. "Come on."

George hauled himself to his feet and pulled Julia up after him. She threw her arms around him, squeezing tightly.

"Come on, come on," the fueler shouted, "Get the hell out of there."

"Let's go," George said. Julia nodded and he guided her past the three agents who were still struggling with Brady, trying to get him handcuffed.

"Let me help with the others," George said to the fueler, once he'd gotten Julia out.

"Yeah, yeah, just hurry up."

As George turned to go back up the aisle, Rick and Jack Haley were already pulling the Judge to his feet. He backed up to let them by. "How is he?"

"Not good," answered Haley. "He needs medical attention."

"That was a hell of thing." Rick worked with Haley to maneuver the Judge through the door. "A hell of a thing." His face was flushed, as if from strenuous exercise.

George looked at his old friend with concern. "Are you okay?"

"Yeah, I'm fine, Georgie. But that was a hell of thing."

Naomi watched from the cockpit as the others left the airplane. Brady was still struggling with the three agents who had invaded the plane, and beyond him, George was ushering the other three men down the steps.

Time to go, she decided. She rose from her seat and made her way back, stepping past the knot of men who were busy subduing Brady. As she did so, a hand snaked out and grabbed her ankle.

Naomi lost her balance and fell onto the pile of men. As if in slow motion, she saw a gun flying from one of the agent's hands and go spinning through the air. It bounced and came to rest next to Brady's head.

That's not a good place for it to be, Naomi thought. She tried to grab the weapon but it was too late: Brady bucked with amazing strength and got an arm free to reach for the gun. The next thing Naomi knew, her world was exploding.

The first bullet smashed through the window on the left side of the cabin. The second blew half of the pilot's head off. The third hit one of the agents in the back as he tried to roll away. Three more bullets went through the cabin ceiling, but the seventh and eighth hit the second agent in the chest. The ninth bullet smashed into the bathroom door, close to where George had been standing—but George wasn't there any more.

Brady kept pulling the trigger long after the gun was out of ammunition. Finally, he heaved his body up. "Get off me," he snarled, but Naomi was beyond rational response by then. All she could do was to scream. Brady rolled hard to his left, until he was free. He sat up, kicking out at Naomi. Then he grabbed one of the other agents' guns.

After the initial burst of gunfire, the interior of the plain went quiet—apart from the sound of Naomi screaming. George found himself on the asphalt at the bottom of the steps. He must have fallen badly as he dived away from the hail of bullets raking the airplane's interior; his shoulder was screaming with white hot bolts of agony.

The others were scuttling under the plane. His eyes sought out Julia. She looked okay. An agent seemed to be ushering them to shelter. Another agent beckoned George to join them, which seemed like an excellent idea. But before he could move, another shot rang out. The bullet punched the ground near his head, showering him with fragments of asphalt.

"Not so fast, Little Wing."

George raised his head. Brady was standing above him, in the doorway. The agent who had beckoned to George, crouching directly under the airplane's belly, wouldn't be able to see. George tried to signal him by flicking his eyes up and down over Brady's position, but the man didn't respond.

"How about you and I going for another little ride?" Brady asked.

"It's over Brady. Even you must be able to see that."

"It's over when I say it's over. Now, get your ass in here and start this thing up." Brady raised his gun and scarred the tarmac again, to make his point.

The agent was waving his gun. He seemed to want George to cooperate. George nodded and scrambled to his feet, wincing as he inadvertently put some weight on his injured shoulder. "We'll never make it out of here, Brady."

"You always were a pessimist, Little Wing. Now get the fuck up here."

George reached the ladder and started up the steps, just as Brady was launched down. George just had time to see Naomi in the doorway before Brady cannoned into him, sending both of them to the ground. George's head impacted the asphalt, and things went a little woozy.

There was a sharp report as the agent under the plane fired. Brady spun round, seemingly unhurt, and pumped off a burst from his nine millimeter. When the echoes of gunfire had dissipated, the agent lay prone under the airplane. The second fueler emerged from under the starboard wing. Brady squeezed off a shot, but missed. The agent retreated behind the Gulfstream, several yards away, his footsteps pounding across the tarmac. Brady squatted, peering underneath the belly of the plane.

Then he turned back toward George, who was still lying on the tarmac, too dazed to move. "You stinking piece of shit." He launched a vicious kick into George's stomach. George grunted with pain and doubled up. Brady kicked him again. "You think you can fuck with Carlos Santez? You think you can fuck with *me?*"

George looked up at his attacker. He couldn't make out Brady's features; everything seemed to be shrouded with mist. Brady's boot lashed out again and again. George tried to twist aside as it crunched into his chest and then his head. His brain exploded with a searing flash of light, and then there was darkness.

Chapter 32

Naomi knew she had to something. She'd thought that it was over, that the agents who'd swarmed into the plane would handle things, but that wasn't how it was going to be. George was getting killed out there, and she was the only one who could do anything about it.

She braced herself in the doorway of the plane, holding one of the fallen agents' guns in both hands. Brady drew back his foot ready to launch another kick at George's head.

Naomi squeezed the trigger.

The impact showered grit over Brady's pants leg. "Don't touch him again, Keyes," she commanded. "Drop that gun, or I swear I'll kill you." The barrel wavered a little: Naomi was familiar with handguns, but she'd never actually contemplated shooting anyone before.

Brady smiled. "Take it easy, Naomi. I'm not going to hurt you."

"Damn right you're not. Put that piece on the ground"

Brady set the gun on the ground. "See? I'm not going to hurt you."

He moved toward the steps. "What do you think the Feds are going to do with you? You think they'll care that you went soft about that Ashton bitch?"

"Stop!"

Brady continued toward the plane. "Trust me, Naomi. I'm the only one who can get us out of this."

"Stop or I'll shoot. I mean it!" Her hands were shaking harder, now.

Brady paused on the steps. "Take it easy. You're in this just as deep as I am. You haven't got a chance without me."

"Naomi, don't listen to him," Julia yelled to her. She had made her way to where George lay and was kneeling next him.

Brady ignored the intrusion, focusing only on Naomi. "Don't listen to her, Naomi, Just hand me the gun." He took another step toward her.

She couldn't bring herself to do it. Trembling, she let the barrel drop. Brady seized his opportunity: he grabbed the gun from her hand, then pushed her back inside the plane.

"That's what I thought. Gutless, just like the rest of these sheep." He looked back at George, who was still lying in a crumpled heap on the ground. "Poor Little Wing. I didn't even need to kill him. He gave up the one chance he had to really live his life, twenty-five years ago."

Julia watched helplessly as Brady pulled up the steps. She ran to the door and started pounding on it. "Goddamn it, Keyes, open up!"

The port engine began turning over. Julia pounded harder. "Let her go, Brady! Please let her go!" The engine began spooling up. The blast from the prop was too much for her, so Julia slid back along the fuselage. She almost tripped over an agent's body.

Haley's Comet began to move, knocking over the ladder in front of the wing. The starboard engine engaged.

Julia crawled over to George. Sobbing, she cradled his head in her hands. "George, please wake up."

He didn't respond. She looked up as *Haley's Comet* turned onto the taxiway to her left. To her right, men were pouring out of the FBO and spreading across the tarmac. Some of them leveled their weapons at the plane. She jumped up and ran toward them. "Don't shoot!" She waved her hands, trying to attract their attention. "Naomi's still on board!" She ran toward the agent who seemed to be directing the others. He glanced at her. "Don't shoot!" she shouted again.

"Hold your fire," ordered the man.

A few seconds later, Julia stumbled into his arms. "Naomi," she said, sobbing between breaths, "Naomi's on the plane."

"Are you sure?"

"Yes."

"Who's flying it?"

"Brady Keyes."

"Can he fly a plane?"

"I don't know," Julia said. "All I know is that I couldn't stop him."

The officer turned to one of his agents. "Get the chopper up and notify Minneapolis Center that we are tracking an aircraft. Make sure those guys know that there's still a hostage on board. Tell them not to interfere with it unless I give the signal."

Haley's Comet continued down the taxiway toward the runway. Two official cars raced to intercept.

Breathing easier, Julia pulled herself away. "I'm sorry."

"It's all right, Mrs. Ashton. I'm Agent Luscomb."

"George is hurt," she said matter of factly. "Can someone help me?"

"We'll take care of him," said Luscomb.

Julia paid no attention. She returned to where George lay. A couple of agents hurried after her. Blue lights flashed in the distance as an ambulance moved onto the tarmac.

For some reason he couldn't understand, George was lying on asphalt and staring at the sky. He seemed to be completely alone, though somewhere nearby an airplane was revving up.

Then Julia was there, tears welling in her eyes as she gazed down. "Try not to move." Her hand was cool on his forehead. "Someone will be here to take care of you in a moment."

George smiled weakly. His head hurt like hell. In fact, his whole body hurt like hell. He tried to sit up so he could check the damage, but Julia pushed him back down. "Try not to move," she said again.

But the sound of the airplane's revving engines was getting stronger. George managed to sit up, wincing with pain. He touched his head and his hand came away sticky with blood. Looking up from his fingers, he saw *Haley's Comet* heading down the runway. "Who's flying the Comet?"

"Brady."

"They're letting him get away!" He started to get to his feet, though it seemed like it was going to take him a while.

"He's got Naomi," Julia said.

Pain rolled over George in waves. He wobbled as he stood, clinging to Julia for support. "Son of a bitch—they've got to stop him! He can't fly that thing!" he said through gritted teeth.

"They can't risk hurting Naomi."

George watched helplessly as *Haley's Comet* gathered speed, fuel from the open tank on the wing spewing out into the slip stream. The pursuing FBI cars were falling back. The airplane's nose rose and the wheels left the ground for an instant before touching back down with a loud chirp.

The nose rose up again, and this time the wheels left the ground and stayed up. The plane slowly gained altitude, but the nose kept pitching up.

"Airspeed, you fool!" exclaimed George. "What the hell are you doing?" Still the nose kept rising. "You're going to stall her!"

The nose abruptly dropped, and *Haley's Comet* rolled to the left as the plane began to dive.

"They're going to crash," Julia said.

The nose kept dropping. As the plane approached the ground, it accelerated further and disappeared behind a tree line. An instant later, a huge fireball lashed toward the sky.

George stood rooted to the spot. The death of *Haley's Comet* had taken mere seconds, but he knew it would haunt his imagination forever. He was still mesmerized by the stricken airplane's final, twisting fall. Julia's voiced seemed far away.

"Naomi was in there," she said quietly.

An FBI helicopter raced toward the crash site. George turned toward his wife, painfully raising his hand to brush the tears from her cheeks. She looked up at him.

He shook his head, unable to find any words of comfort. He was almost relieved when Luscomb and several of his men came running up.

"Get that ambulance over here, now!" Luscomb snapped. He turned to George. "What happened?"

"Brady. He went for a gun," George answered, grimacing with the pain. "Before I knew what was happening, the pilot was dead and Carr and Howard were down. Things got out of control. Naomi tried to stop him, but—"

"Why would she have done that?"

"She was helping us," said Julia.

"Why?"

"I guess she came to see Roy and Brady for what they were. But you'd have to ask her."

Luscomb glanced toward the crash site, marked by a pall of thick, oily smoke. "It appears we won't be able to that now."

"Yes, it does," Julia said.

"Was Keyes a pilot?"

"He told me he'd had some experience in Santez's planes," George said. "He knew a little about flying, but I doubt he ever soloed in a King Air."

Rick trotted up. "Holy shit, George. What happened?"

George turned. "It's finally over, old friend."

"Man, I knew it might get heavy, but I never thought it would come to this."

George smiled weakly. "Must have been our karma."

"You don't suppose Naomi had anything to do with that, do you?" Rick asked.

"I don't know, old buddy. I guess we'll never know."

Chapter 33

Most of the trees on the street were in full bloom, basking in the warm sun of a beautiful late spring day and giving up their fresh green scent to the air. The big oaks still had the fewest leaves. Last to green up in the spring and first to turn in the fall, George thought. Maybe that's why they grew so slowly.

"You know, this is my favorite time of the year," he said.

Julia was driving, keeping her speed down and trying to avoid the bumps that brought winces to George's face. "So you often say," she said, just a hint of sarcasm in her voice.

Neighbors were out in full force, doing yard work or just taking advantage of the weather. One smiled and waved. George waved back absently. "Isn't that Mrs. Hoffman?" he asked. "I didn't think she knew I existed."

"She does now," said Julia. "And so does everyone else since you've been plastered all over the news."

They passed Phil Lukich, mowing his lawn as usual, just before they pulled into their driveway. Phil stopped his mower and headed over to greet them.

"Oh shit! Here comes Phil," George said, as Phil came running up to the car.

"He's been dying to see you. He must have asked me twenty times when you'd be home."

"Georgie, baby, the neighborhood hero!" Phil opened the door for George.

"Hi, Phil." George climbed out of his seat, moving gingerly.

"You okay?" Phil asked. "Let me help you."

"Thanks. I'll be all right."

"Man, I just can't believe it. My buddy rescuing a Federal Judge from an international drug gang. What a story!"

"Julia had a little to do with it, too, you know." George stood aside to let Phil shut the car door. "Although you wouldn't know it from the papers."

"I thought so." Phil bent over to give Julia a peck on the cheek as she came over to help George. "She was pretty coy when I talked to her yesterday, but I didn't think you could have pulled off something like that without some help from the brains of the outfit."

"I couldn't have," George said sincerely.

"Here, lean on me, buddy," said Phil as they started toward the house.

"I can walk," George said. All around, neighbors who had been busy with yard work stopped what they were doing to watch the homecoming. "Damn, this is embarrassing."

"Get used to it. You're going to be the center of attention for a while."

"I wonder how friendly they'll be if I end up being prosecuted for flying across international borders illegally, or interfering with Canadian and US officials, or breaking about a hundred FAA regulations, or a host of other infractions I've been threatened with."

"No way, man. You saved a Judge." Phil chuckled. "I mean, who are they gonna get to convict you?"

"Well, there's still going to be a shitload of trouble before things get back to normal."

As they reached the door, George turned to Phil. "Thanks for your help, neighbor, but it's been a long week."

"Oh, yeah, sure. Look, I'm outta here. You guys let me know if you need anything."

Before he could go, Julia touched his shoulder, saying, "We appreciate all your support, Phil. We'll get together for dinner in a day or two."

"Absolutely." Phil gave Julia another peck on the cheek before leaving. "See you soon."

As they went inside, Julia said, "He's a good neighbor. You can't imagine how concerned he was about you."

George smiled, "He can be a pain in the ass sometimes, but he really is okay."

He stood in his living room. Everything was the same, but it all seemed to be in sharper focus, rich with details that he usually ignored. Julia watched as he went around the room, inspecting pictures and running his hands over the furniture, studying tiny nicks in the woodwork. He paused at the fish tank and sprinkled some food on the water, and waited as the ripples spread and the fish came to feed.

Luscomb had come to visit him in the hospital, the night before. It seemed that Judge Strand was still in intensive care, but he was expected to be all right. Jack Haley had provided testimony that would be a great help to all the rescuers in any upcoming legal snarls.

The official FBI report stated Brady's death was caused by the crash, but there was a gash in the back of his head that was inconsistent with the crash signature—and Naomi's remains had been recovered from the cockpit area, not the passenger compartment.

Julia broke his reverie. "Strange, isn't it? Seems as though we've been gone for years, instead of days."

He nodded slowly, watching the serenity of the fish in their tank. "Do you think they even noticed we were gone?"

Julia came over and encircled his waist with her arm. "I don't think they can hold on to memories for more than a few seconds."

"I wonder if that would be a blessing or a curse."

"Depends. Some memories we'd give anything to let go of. Others are so precious that we want to relive them."

"I guess that's the price of being human."

She turned to face him. "George, we've both been through a terrible ordeal, but don't go getting morose on me."

"It seems so strange, though. Like, it was destiny that we

should eventually pay for our sins of the past but for some reason I survived. Why?"

"If it's destiny, you should accept it graciously."

George thought about that for a moment. "I suppose. If it had gone the other way, I wouldn't have had much choice, would I?" He fell silent. She stood next to him, waiting. "I'm sorry," he said at last. "I guess the thought processing is a little slow. Must be the medication."

Julia squeezed his hand. "It's going to take some time to get back to normal. I feel it too. But we'll work through it together."

George smiled at her. He lifted her hand to his lips and kissed it.

Printed in the United States
62105LVS00001B/52-99

9 781905 605095